UNDERCOVER JUSTICE

NICO ROSSO

For Ami.

Chapter One

Stephanie Shun didn't steal cars. Her father had always told her if there was a car she wanted that someone wasn't willing to sell, there were people they could hire to steal it for her. But she'd stopped listening to him long ago, around the time she decided that his criminal empire tucked into a corner of Chinatown, San Francisco, wasn't the legacy she wanted to be buried under.

And yet here she was, crouched next to a car in a dark parking lot, prying the plastic cover off the side-view mirror. To anyone who might catch her, it would look like she was a car thief, and that was exactly what she wanted. This job was the first step to ingratiating herself with a crew of drivers who contracted out to the worst criminals on the West Coast, and it had to look perfect. Nobody could know she was stealing her own car.

Once she had the side-view mirror cover separated out enough to spot a collection of thin wires, she placed a plastic wedge in the gap and pulled a multi-tool from her belt. Even if it was her car, bought and paid for with the profits from her various investments, it was still a crime to threaten the bodywork of the sleek Mercedes. Striving to minimize any exterior damage, she selected one of the wires and stripped the insulation from a section using the knife of the multi-tool.

Footsteps froze her. It was after three o'clock in the

morning, and still someone was up on the second floor of the private parking lot to retrieve their car. One of the hazards of committing crimes in a city as populated as San Francisco: there was activity at all hours. She coiled her body by the front wheel, in case anyone was searching below the chassis. The buzzing lights on the concrete ceiling created deep shadows for her to hide in. She knew she was undetected by the security camera, but an individual might spot her, even though she wore all black and carried a black bag.

The quick pace of the footsteps put her mind at ease. A guard would've been less direct, but this person had no intention of lingering in the parking lot. They got into their car and closed the door. Stephanie used the sound of the engine starting to mask her retrieving an electronic device from her bag. Headlights turned on three rows over, making her shift her feet so they were in the shadow of the wheel next to her.

But the other car didn't move. Checking their phone? Waiting for the heater to kick in? The night was cold, but Stephanie shivered with a deeper chill. Her watch read 3:21 a.m. The instruction from the driving crew boss was that she had to have a stolen car on the road by 3:30 a.m., when he would text her the next move. If she botched this job, it would kill her chances to get in with the crew. And if that happened, the ultimate target could slip through her fingers.

This was the one shot to find human traffickers who'd eluded law enforcement for too long. And while Stephanie had access to the law's resources, she didn't have to play by their rules. That was the point of re-forming Frontier Justice over a hundred years after her ancestor had first helped create the organization. The vigilante group wasn't exactly legal then, or now, giving her the space she needed to go after the bad guys.

The other car in the parking lot finally chugged into

gear and crept up the aisle. It was a risk, but the clock was ticking, so she resumed her work on stealing the Mercedes before the other car completely descended this level. She attached a small metal clip to the exposed wire in the side-view mirror and plugged that into the electronic device in her hand. The dim screen immediately started scrolling with information taken from the central computer of the coupe. Pushing buttons on the side of the screen narrowed the focus of the data scan until she located the factory-set key codes for the car.

She adjusted a mode switch on the side of the handmade device, pressed another button to broadcast the captured code and the doors to the Mercedes unlocked. Of course, she could've done all that with the key fob that sat in her Pacific Heights condo, but that wouldn't make this theft look legit to the driving crew.

After detaching the clip from the wire and replacing the side-view mirror cover to a near-perfect standard, she eased open the passenger-side door and pushed her bag into the footwell. She climbed over the seat and slid behind the steering wheel. A press of the button on the dash brought the Mercedes purring to life.

She was going to miss driving this car. Undoubtedly, once she delivered it to the driving crew they'd replace the VIN and sell it on the black market. All the registration paperwork was tied to a shell company she owned that could never be traced back to her, thus maintaining her reputation for the criminals.

The sleek two-door coupe slithered from its parking spot and down the aisle. She checked her watch; still on time. Barely. As she eased the car down the circular ramp, she wondered if maybe she should've stolen her Audi that was parked one floor away. Or the Subaru tuned for street racing in her condo garage. But as much as she loved the handling of the coupe, she was ready to move on from this

Mercedes. One of the last passengers she'd had was a first date that had fizzled as soon as the tech entrepreneur's eyes had lit up while asking her about her father. It wasn't the first time a man was more interested in dating Eddie Shun's daughter rather than seeing her as simply Stephanie Shun.

All for the best, she sighed to herself. She'd gotten her thrills collecting the pieces to Frontier Justice and shooting at armed guards on a multimillion-dollar estate near San Jose during their very first mission. The first mission of this century, at least.

And there was no way that date would've acted as lookout while she'd stolen her own car.

She drove to the front gate of the parking lot, which lifted automatically, and slipped through, casually using her hand to obscure her face for the security cameras. Any guard there would've recognized her, but the whole gambit had to be airtight. If the information Frontier Justice had collected from police and FBI communications, as well as underworld rumors, was correct, the driving crew was tied to human trafficking run by the Seventh Syndicate, and those bastards didn't miss a detail.

One block away from the parking garage, the phone she'd bought and set up for this mission buzzed with a text from the head of the driving crew, Ronald Olesk. She'd never actually met Olesk, but had made contact through a friend of a friend of a friend. The message was simple. A time and address.

"Son of a…" Tension rang in tight coils up her spine. She had ten minutes to get there. At this time of night, it shouldn't be a problem. The real trouble was the address. It was a warehouse owned by her father.

THE LAST TIME Arash Shamshiri had robbed someone, he thought he was going to die. Maybe not that night, but he'd known that if he'd continued with that life he would've wound up with a bullet in him. Yet here he was, letting his muscle memory take over as he picked the lock to an office on the second floor of a warehouse catwalk.

He'd already cased the patterns of the guards from an upper window. Dim lights high in the warehouse turned everything into a mosaic of black and green. He'd creaked the window open during a gust of wind that had made the whole building groan. Climbing across girders and down steel supports had been the easy part. Now he was on the same level as three of the guards, scraping his old lock picks against the tumblers and knowing any second there would be shouting followed by shooting.

Luckily he hadn't completely lost his touch and the lock gave way. The guards were at the farthest point of their rounds. He opened the door just wide enough to slide inside the office. Breathing slow in an attempt to keep his heart from pounding out of his chest, he crouched among the desks and file cabinets. Somewhere in this mess was the single piece of paper he'd been tasked to find.

It was a test. He'd known that when the instructions arrived in a text from Ronald Olesk. But it was a test he couldn't fail. Arash knew how these gangs worked: prove yourself and you were in the door. Keep proving yourself and you gained their trust.

Once those murderers thought he was one of their own, he could strike.

But before he could think about revenge, he had to find the schedule for Eddie Shun's produce trucks. The most up-to-date one would be on the top of any stack. From the way the broccoli and brussels sprouts were smelling on the warehouse floor, it was time to move them out. The drivers would probably arrive in just a couple of hours.

He checked a clock on the wall. Damn, it had taken longer to get into the office than he anticipated. The text from Olesk had been very specific. Arash was to get to the location on foot. His ride away from the warehouse would be arriving at 3:40 a.m. and departing before 3:41 a.m. He had four minutes to find the piece of paper and get to the street.

Panicking wouldn't get this job done. He focused on the space. He'd been a truck driver before, making predawn deliveries while working his way through trade school. Manifests and schedules were always flying through these offices. The large desk at the center was the hub. He crept there and craned his head up to look over the surface.

The first thing he saw was one of the guards walking past the safety-glass windows that made up one side of the offices. Arash froze and his pulse thundered in his ears. He knew if he ducked out of the way too quickly the movement would tip the guard off. The man's silhouette continued past the windows, then around another stretch of the catwalks.

Arash eased out a breath and refocused on the desk. Askew on one corner was a clipboard. Its grease-stained edges showed that it had traveled from the warehouse floor and back up to these offices. Keeping his eyes on the front windows, he stretched his arm out and snatched the clipboard back.

The content on the page was illegibly dark. He had a very powerful flashlight in his jacket pocket, but that would surely alert every guard in the place that he was picking through their business. He got as low as he could and crept toward the front windows to let the warehouse light bring the text into focus. The date at the top was today and the shipping times were all laid out in a grid with truck numbers and cargo.

Arash released the page from the clipboard and folded it into his jacket. He replaced the clipboard on the desk, then returned to the front door of the offices. The clock on the wall told him he had two minutes to meet his ride out of there. Not enough time to sneak his way back up to the roof. Hell, there wasn't enough time to walk out the front door.

He stood up and opened the door to the office. He had to run, right past the guards.

STEPHANIE HADN'T WORN any rings, in case they'd caught the light and given her away while stealing her car, but now she wished she'd brought at least one so she could release a fraction of the tension by twisting it around her finger.

Her mother had always hated the habit. She'd wanted Stephanie to pick one set of jewelry and wear only that to demark her presence in the world. Changing it out every week had kept her grounded, though. A variety of rings felt differently on her fingers, making her focus on her hands. She hadn't been ready to define herself as a teenager straining against a family and lifestyle she hadn't chosen, and still wasn't.

3:40 a.m. If her pickup wasn't here in the next minute, she had to leave. Whoever they were, why the hell hadn't they been early? Every second that ticked by with her parked in the shadows near her father's warehouse was another opportunity for doom. If he found her there, her cover would be blown. And she had to operate with the confidence that Olesk and his crew had no idea who she was.

A side door on the warehouse slammed open. She jumped, startled, then quickly gathered her composure and put the car in gear. She'd stolen the ride, and now her job was getaway driver. A single figure sprinted onto the sidewalk, then toward her as she approached. Shadows enveloped him; she couldn't pick out any of his features. He reached the car and threw open the passenger door.

Just then, two more men emerged from the warehouse door. One of them limped. Both held pistols. Her pickup leaped into the car and slammed the door closed. "Get us out of here." He didn't yell, but his urgency was unmistakable.

Not that she needed encouragement. The two armed

guards were enough. She hit the gas and zipped past them before they could bring their guns up. The car handled the next corner perfectly and they were quickly away from the warehouse.

Her passenger was twisted around in his seat to watch the rear. When he turned to the front, she could finally steal a look at his face. Intense dark eyes peered forward. Black hair was pulled back into a short ponytail, accentuating his chiseled cheekbones and pronounced nose. He had a trim goatee. His mouth was set in a grim line. She guessed he was Middle Eastern, and honestly would've been happy to spend more time examining this handsome thirtysomething-year-old man's distinctive features, but the street curved ahead again. And he was a member of a criminal driving crew she was intent on taking down.

He turned again to scan beside and behind them, bringing his shoulder and broad chest close to her in the small coupe. His body was covered in black clothes, but the cords of his neck and the energy that radiated from him showed how strong he was.

"Damn it..." he growled.

"Did you get what you went there for?" She couldn't allow this job to go sideways and ruin her chance with Olesk.

"Of course I did," he shot back. "Why do you think I was running away?"

"Then what's the problem?"

"Three cars with their headlights off following us are the problem." He pointed to a street parallel to theirs. Two sport-tuned compact cars and a high-end sedan prowled into an intersection, then veered directly toward Stephanie and her passenger.

She sneered, "Awesome," and stood on the accelerator. Her passenger tugged his seat belt on and braced himself against the door frame. They zipped through the flat streets of the Dogpatch neighborhood, but she couldn't shake the pursuers. "What's your name?" she asked through a clenched jaw.

"Arash." He continued to turn, tracking the other cars.

"Okay, Arash, in the side pocket of my bag at your feet is a transponder." If this man was skilled enough to steal something from Eddie Shun, then he should be able to figure it out. Though he wasn't so masterful that he got out of the warehouse undetected.

He pulled the bag into his lap and dived into the side. "Got it." Holding the device up, he said, impressed, "These things are expensive."

"Who says I bought it?" In fact, she had, from a third-party contact she had in the black market.

"Slick." His gaze scanned her for a moment and she thought she detected a quick heat of attraction. It inspired an unexpected bloom of warmth across her chest. The two of them raced over the San Francisco streets and for the first time in a long time, she felt a little reckless. She shut it down immediately and focused on the road. Arash cooled, as well. He turned to the device in his hands. "You used this to get the Mercedes?" His thick fingers traced up the lead wire with the metal clip. "Picked up the key code from the CAN bus in the main computer."

"Can you operate it?" There was no time to walk him through. The other cars were gaining, and she was going to run out of streets and wind up in the bay within a few blocks.

"Get me close." He clicked over the device, and her quick glance told her he was setting it up to give the oncoming sedan a false key code. Like he'd read her mind.

"Ready?" She eased off the gas enough to allow the oncoming cars to close the gap.

"One second." He continued to adjust the transponder. Her composure threatened to crack. The cars were too close. Sweat chilled her arms. If any of those guards saw her, they'd know who she was. And if she screwed up this job, her chance to infiltrate Olesk's crew would be ruined. "Time's up."

"I'm good." Arash held up the device and looked out the back window. "Closer. We have to be within—"

"Three feet," she finished for him. "I know."

"Then put us in the sweet spot," he clipped. One of the sports cars broke off from the formation to flank her. The other held tight to the closing sedan. She slowed, her heart racing, until the sedan nearly brushed her back bumper.

"Not yet!" she called out. Before Arash could question her, she yanked the steering wheel to the right and commanded, "Now!"

Arash hit the button as the sedan was swerving to adjust to her sudden move. The riding lights flashed on the sedan, then the car went dead. The sports car that had been next to it couldn't get out of the way in time and jammed into the side of the sedan. Both the cars ground to a stop. Arash barked a harsh laugh of victory. "I have to get one of these."

"Don't steal mine." She shared a glance with him, again shocked by the heat in the brief look. Was she turned on? No. Not by a criminal.

"Broadcasted key codes won't work on the tuner." He jammed the transceiver back into her bag. "Totally different security system." One car remained on their trail. Her action with the sedan had slowed her down enough for it to keep a steady pace now. And it was gaining.

She sped through the streets, hugging corners and scanning ahead for anything she could use to stop the other car. Arash reached into his jacket and pulled out a dark metal object. Ice spiked through her nerves. "We don't need a gun," she growled. Whoever was chasing them was an employee of her father. While his businesses weren't 100 percent legal, they also didn't involve the kinds of crimes that hurt people. Like human trafficking.

To prove what she said, she navigated quickly into an alley and gained ground on the last car. Arash answered, "I'm not packing on this run." He displayed the object in his hand, a heavy-duty flashlight. "But I can still punch back." The passenger window glided down, blasting cold, briny air into the car. He leaned out the window and extended the flashlight back. Suddenly the alley behind her was filled with bright white strobing light.

The next street arrived and she steered hard to the left. The driver behind must've been dazzled by the strobe, because the sports car turned early and jammed its nose into the side of a building. Metal and plastic crunched. The last car was out of the race.

But she didn't let off the speed until they'd slipped completely out of the neighborhood. Easing into the flow of the few cars on the road, she started to drive like a civilian. Arash rolled up the window and gave her an approving nod. "Nice wheel work."

"Nice work riding shotgun." It was way too easy to flirt with this man. This criminal.

Arash's crooked smile disappeared into a thin line when he pulled out his buzzing phone. "Text from Olesk." Her awareness sharpened. Nerves prickled. The first test was a success. What was next? Arash continued, "It's the address where we're to meet him." His dark gaze stared ahead. His voice was low and serious. "We have two hours to get to Sacramento."

The gravity of the message shook deep into her bones. The mission for Frontier Justice had started, and the only way to go was forward. Olesk and his crew were out there waiting, and she was headed right toward them with one of their own riding next to her.

She steered the car toward a highway, already past the point of no return.

Chapter Two

Arash's hands itched without a steering wheel in them. His foot pressed against the floor of the Mercedes, even though there was no gas pedal beneath it. He always drove. Not that the woman in the driver's seat couldn't. She'd handled the machine like she was part of it.

His pulse was still racing, even though they'd long lost their pursuers and were on the dark highway to Sacramento. Damn, but it had been sexy to see her pretty lips curled into a sneer as she bared her teeth during the chase. Her dark eyes had somehow remained cool while she'd assessed the road ahead and the cars coming after them. The sleek angles of her black bob haircut fit her perfectly.

He hadn't been thinking about any of this while Eddie Shun's men were bearing down on them. But once they were in the clear, he'd been hit by the charged thrill of watching her drive and how they'd worked very well together. Too well.

"I didn't get your name." He couldn't find many personal details looking at the Asian woman who seemed to be around his age. No jewelry. Her manicure was neutral. Even her black, military-style jacket was lacking any logos or brands.

"Stephanie." She kept both her hands on the steering wheel, not offering one to shake.

"Good to be riding with you." He leaned back in the seat

but couldn't get any calm to sink into his muscles. The car rocketed through the night, toward a fight he couldn't wait to start, but he didn't know how or when. He wasn't driving. This badass woman was, he kept reminding himself, part of the gang he was going to destroy. It took some effort to keep his voice casual. "Been rolling with Olesk long?"

"First gig." Her cautious gaze pierced Arash for a split second, then returned to the black highway.

The information resonated like a gunshot. He tried to use it to shape more of what he knew of Stephanie, but he couldn't find enough pieces to bolt together. She could've been lying, but that would be found out as soon as they arrived at Olesk's place. He examined the angles of telling her his own truth and couldn't find any reason not to reveal just a little. "Mine, too."

"Have you met Olesk?" This time when she assessed him there was a little surprise in her eyes.

"Nothing face-to-face." Tension hummed in his spine, not knowing what he was going to do when he was finally in the same room with the man responsible for Marcos's death.

"So we're both on the trial run." She looked him over again, and he felt like she might have X-ray vision the way she took him apart. "What did they send you into the warehouse for?"

He took the piece of paper from his coat and unfolded it. "Shipping orders for today. From Eddie Shun, no less."

She clicked her tongue, nodding, impressed. "You managed to do it."

"And you got me out of there." He put the paper away.

"We passed this test."

So she was heading into the unknown, too. Her face was unreadable in the dash lights. "Olesk will be lucky to have you on the crew. Where'd you learn to push a V8 biturbo like that?"

"I went to private school with a bunch of rich kids." A sly smile crossed her lips. "There were a lot of expensive cars to wreck." She kept her eyes on the road ahead. "But their parents still never paid attention." When she finally turned to him, it was to blink slowly with that smile still on her face. He saw the truth of her words within her nonchalant attitude. And something else, deeper in her look. What she'd seen, and lived, still dwelled in her. He found himself drawn to that depth, wanting to discover what it was she'd learned from her side of life.

"You picked a winner." Before he stared at her too long, he snapped himself back to the moment and ran his hand over the dashboard.

"I'd cased it for a couple days and it hadn't moved out of its parking spot." She patted the steering wheel. "Machine like this needs to run."

And Stephanie seemed like the perfect person to own the streets with the sleek beast. "And clean." He opened the glove compartment and found only the normal paperwork. There wasn't a fast-food napkin in sight. The floor mats in the back seat looked like they'd never been touched by the sole of a shoe. "Whoever's car this is, she was... meticulous."

"How do you know it was a woman?" she challenged.

"Perfume." The dark spiced aroma had hit him once he'd been able to breathe easily after the chase. "It's different from yours."

"I'm not wearing any."

"Your soap, then." The cabin of the car suddenly seemed especially small. Intimate. Like he'd had his face close to the skin of her neck.

She rubbed her thumb along the side of her finger in a slow meditation, then abruptly stopped to grip the steering wheel. Her gaze remained forward. "Breaking and entering, theft, perfuming. What else can you do?"

"I can drive anything with wheels. Tear it down and build it back up again." Was he bragging or flirting? "If it has a motor, I can make it sing." Stick to bragging, he scolded himself. There was no room for a hookup with this woman in his plans for Olesk and Olesk's crew.

"Bet you didn't learn all that in private school."

"I've been seriously in the grease since I was fifteen." Marcos had been right next to him. Until addiction and the need for easy cash pulled Marcos away, leading him ultimately to Olesk. And his death.

"When I can afford one of these—" she tapped the gearshift "—I'll call you to work on it."

He laughed, again the car feeling smaller than before. The early-morning hour seemed to dress a heavy curtain around these moments with the mysterious Stephanie. "A ride this fine never comes into the shop where I wrench. Only mechanics with white coveralls and stainless-steel calipers are qualified to tune these machines."

"So if we break down out here in the middle of nowhere, you couldn't fix it?"

"Hell, yeah, I could." As long as it wasn't the computer brain. "I'll bet you could, too." He pulled the transceiver out of the side pocket of her bag. He'd only heard of these multithousand-dollar devices used to break into the most tech-heavy cars, and had never handled one. It was clearly made on someone's bench, but it was solid and had already proven itself.

"I know my way around combustion." Stephanie shrugged and ran a fingernail down the edge of her bob, straightening it along the side of her cheek.

Now he wanted to see her wiping her greasy hands on a rag while standing over a purring engine. His own heart started thumping at the rate of the fantasy pistons until he shoved the transceiver back into the bag and tried to erase the image from his head. "What other gear is in here? Police radio scrambler? Attack drone?" He hauled the bag into his lap.

"Changes of clothes." She grabbed the bag and slid it into the back seat. "Private changes of clothes."

The tenuous intimacy cooled. "So you knew we'd be road-tripping?" She'd said this was her first gig for Olesk, but that didn't mean she wasn't tighter with the man and his crew than Arash was.

She shook her head. "I prepared for a few possibilities." Her eyes assessed him with some disappointment. "You didn't."

He straightened his jacket and crossed his arms. Flashlight, knife, multi-tool, the cell phone he'd set up specifically for contacting Olesk. Not much else. "I've been focused on other things." Like how to get into the gang without anyone knowing he was really there to destroy it.

"Plan ahead." Stephanie settled in her seat, still alert, but not driving like they were being chased.

He'd always sucked at chess. His father had tried to teach him a couple of times, but he'd always been better at the backgammon games with his mother. More chance. Thinking on the fly. But Stephanie was right. Olesk had to be smart to operate a crew for this long without getting caught. Arash had to be smarter. He gave her a small salute. "Eight moves ahead." One hour until Sacramento. Two hours until sunrise. He had to be ready for Olesk and anything else. That meant not getting twisted up in an attraction with a woman getaway driver. It didn't matter that they'd handled the trouble in San Francisco perfectly, like dancing to the same rhythm. Stephanie was still the enemy.

Two hours driving through the early morning in a "stolen" car with Arash had stripped the insulation from her defenses. The chase through San Francisco hadn't rattled her as much as the cautious conversations they'd used to learn about each other. Not that either was revealing all their truths. She knew he was hiding as much of himself as she was, though he probably wasn't working secretly for an underground vigilante group. But she kept having to remind herself that this man, who listened with interest when she spoke, was part of the evil she was tasked with defeating.

"The next right." Arash's low, gravelly voice was more suited to the bedroom. He'd navigated them off the highway and toward a generic Sacramento suburb. The light from his phone revealed weary eyes. He took a long breath and sat up straighter, rallying. More life shined in his expression as he scanned the area.

She reset her focus. A new day was about to begin. She was about to meet Olesk. Any mistakes she made now would be deadly.

The workday around them had started before the sun, with cars and trucks and vans already on the road. The neighborhood she turned into seemed like it was still sleeping. Lights off. Cars cold. She tried to predict which house was her target but couldn't make any of them seem more criminal than another. Olesk was slick.

But not perfect. "I see it." She aimed for a two-story house covered in taupe stucco. A pickup truck parked on the street in front of it had a wider stance than what rolled off the factory floor.

Arash chuckled. "You're good." He put his phone away. "Someone threw some spacers on their pickup wheels."

"The only nonstock car on the block." She slowed the Mercedes and turned into the driveway. As soon as they crossed the sidewalk, the garage door opened. A line of white light widened ahead, until the space inside the two-car garage was completely exposed. A sport-tuned compact import car took up one spot.

"I hope they have a real shop to work in." Arash cocked his head with a disapproving frown.

She pulled in next to the cluttered workbench, with only basic tools and a scattering of bottles of motor oil and detailing supplies. If Olesk and his crew were breaking down cars, they were doing it somewhere else. Nothing in the garage seemed illegal. Stacks of boxes, a rolling rack hanging with clothes covered in plastic. All perfectly normal to anyone who might be driving or walking past when the door was open.

The Mercedes purred to a stop and she shut it down. She didn't have a moment to take a breath with the resting car before the garage door started closing behind her and Arash. He swung out of the car and faced a door at the back of the garage. She could see that the car ride hadn't locked him up too much. His body was balanced, ready.

She took her time, collecting her bag from the back seat before getting out of her Mercedes one last time.

The door at the back of the garage opened. A tall white man in his thirties with shaggy blond hair filled the frame. His head was cocked to one side confidently, like he was looking at a piece of art he already understood. While his smile was friendly enough, if a little aloof, his eyes were hard. When he stepped down into the garage, Stephanie saw that a woman stood behind him. Blunt bangs dyed dark blue and a high black ponytail. This white woman in her late twenties didn't move into the garage, but stared long, her mouth a thin line.

"Arash, Stephanie." The man moved closer, hand extended. "Ronald Olesk." Arash stepped to him and shook his hand. Stephanie did the same, happy it was just a brusque gesture, without a lingering touch. Olesk checked his watch. "Right on time." His smile cooled. "Heard there was a little extra rubber laid on the ground."

"We handled it." Arash shrugged it off.

Stephanie tipped her chin up, not backing down from Olesk. "Just a little something to get the blood flowing."

The first step of her mission was in play. Now that she knew this location, she could start to put a target on Olesk's back. But taking him down wouldn't give her what she ultimately wanted. This deadly game wasn't going to end quickly.

"You have good taste." Olesk put his hands on his hips and assessed the Mercedes.

"I do." She nudged the car with her hip, sorry to see it go.

The woman in the doorway craned her neck to look in. "Did you nick the fob off of someone?" She had an English accent and a judgmental sneer.

Stephanie answered as dryly as she could. "I pulled the factory key code off the CAN bus."

"She's got the tech." Arash hooked a thumb toward Stephanie with a grin. "Thing of beauty." His energy was so different than the other two. Comfortable and loose, he didn't have to posture to prove he was tough.

The woman in the doorway narrowed her eyes on Stephanie, ignoring Arash. Olesk chuckled and said to Stephanie, "You'll have to show Ellie that trick."

"After some sleep." It might be Olesk's crew, but she didn't have to act like a minion.

"Of course." Olesk waved his hand toward the doorway. Ellie slipped away into the house. Stephanie stepped first to the door. As Arash passed Olesk, the blond man put his hand out. "You have my paperwork?"

Arash pulled the folded page from his jacket and slapped it into Olesk's palm. It might've just been early-morning frayed nerves, but the move seemed somewhat aggressive to Stephanie, though Arash kept the smile in his eyes. If Olesk felt it the way she did, he didn't show it.

Olesk unfolded the paper and looked it over, nodding. "You guys deliver good stuff."

Arash picked up one of the empty bottles of motor oil from the workbench as he passed it. "I hope you didn't bring me here just to do oil changes." He tossed the bottle back; it clunked against the others, knocking them over in a noise too loud for this hour of the morning.

Olesk stopped walking and both Stephanie and Arash turned to him. Warning tension prickled up her spine. Her back was to the open doorway where Ellie had disappeared. Olesk ran his hand through his hair in what appeared to be a practiced move. "We're the Slick Track Racers," he explained. "Anyone mentions STR and you know that we're the best at stealing cars, breaking down cars, fixing them up, moving them without being caught." He took a dramatic pause. "Sometimes we do oil changes. Sometimes we get paid a lot of money to get someone's merchandise from one place to another without a scratch, and without anyone knowing anything about it."

She forced a casual look on her face while her blood boiled. The merchandise he was talking about were human beings, people trafficked by the Seventh Syndicate.

"I'm here for all that." Arash nodded with approval, lowering her opinion of him.

"Good." Olesk waved them toward the doorway again and they all moved into a featureless mudroom. "Because we need reliable people for a very important gig." They passed a laundry room, then emerged into the kitchen. Empty packages of convenience food were stacked on the counters. There was no aroma of fresh cooking. "We had a problem with a conscience." Olesk drew a horizontal line in the air with a long finger, as if demarking a border. "And we don't want those."

Ellie emerged from the other side of the kitchen with two white envelopes. She handed them to Stephanie and Arash, eyes still wary.

Olesk pointed at their envelopes. "Work solid, get paid." Stephanie sneaked a peek into the envelope and riffled across eighty hundred-dollar bills. Anger continued to simmer beneath her skin. Blood money. The big gig he was talking about was what she really wanted. Then the STR and the Seventh Syndicate could go down in flames. Olesk walked them farther into the house. Few pieces of furniture littered the tan carpet, just enough to crash comfortably for a few hours. "Thom and Hector are sleeping. You'll meet them tomorrow after they finish their assignments." He stopped at an open doorway in an undecorated hallway. "This is you." He pointed at Stephanie. "Bathroom's down here. And on the other side's Arash." Wrapping his arm around Ellie's hip, he ambled toward a flight of carpeted stairs. "We're upstairs. Get your rest, take the morning off, get outfitted. Expect to move." He sent Stephanie and Arash a wave as he ascended the stairs. Ellie didn't look in their direction.

Arash stood outside his room for a second and turned to Stephanie. "Good night."

"Good morning," she answered wryly and stepped into her room. The door closed securely and luckily had a lock. Still, she wedged the back of a small chair under the handle. Arash's last word wrapped around her like a thick blanket, muting sound and making her think about a possibility of meeting this man who seemed to balance easily with her somewhere where they weren't surrounded by a criminal gang. Meeting him in a different life, when he wasn't part of that same gang.

She sat on the bed and took out her phone. There were no details of her real self anywhere in the device. It would be so easy to send a text to Ty, Mariana and Vincent, the other members of Frontier Justice, to let them know where she was and that she'd made the first move into Olesk's gang. Any kind of lifeline or reminder that she wasn't alone. But if anyone in this house caught sight of that contact, she'd be dead.

The narrow mattress creaked as she stretched out, shoes still on. She dug her phone charger out of her bag and plugged it in. It rested on the small nightstand, next to the slim automatic pistol she laid within reach.

Thick curtains covered the one north-facing window. They should be enough to block the coming day. Still, she knew there was only time for a couple hours of sleep. This house wasn't set up for long breaks, and Olesk's energy revealed there were plans in the works.

Her heavy bones sank her deeper into the bed. She convinced herself not to worry about the sleep she was going to miss, and just to concentrate on the rest she felt in that moment. For now, she was alone. Despite the ease with which she and Arash worked together, he couldn't be trusted. Frontier Justice was miles away, and she couldn't call them in until she was much closer to her ultimate target. Her life was on the line to help others, just like her nineteenth-century ancestor on her mother's side. Li Jie had emigrated from China to the American West, worked in the mines, lived through the collapses and dynamite and the racism. Many people had seen him as less than human, and legally he couldn't testify against a white man in court, yet still he had the strength to help form the first Frontier Justice and fight for others who suffered under that same oppression.

He'd survived. Now she must do the same, to save countless people from Olesk and the Seventh Syndicate.

ARASH NEEDED TO SLEEP, but all he wanted to do was tear down the walls of the house around him. A man snored steadily in the next room. Arash would never feel that calm, that safe, until he knew that Olesk and the STR were wiped off the face of the earth.

Had Marcos been in this room? Lying on the mattress on the floor, resting between gigs for the gang? Olesk said he'd had a problem with a conscience. Arash knew who he'd been talking about. Marcos had been found dead in a car wreck on the highway south of Livermore. Arash hadn't seen the body, but he'd found the twisted car in the scrap yard. And he'd tracked down the spot where it had happened. It wasn't an accident. It was murder. Another car's paint scraped into the side of Marcos's vehicle. Tire tracks revealed the moment of impact, perfectly timed to send Marcos into the concrete pillar of an overpass.

Recounting all this wasn't the way to get to sleep. Arash's heart thundered with anger, thinking about his friend's last race toward freedom. He'd texted Arash that night and asked for help. Marcos was finally looking for a way out of the spiral he'd gotten into. But forever after that text, that last contact, was…silence.

Arash took a long breath and focused his memory on Stephanie's hands. Her fine fingers were so sure as she steered the Mercedes through the chase. Remembering her movements helped bring a bit of a hypnotic calm. He knew he shouldn't be thinking of her this way. She couldn't be trusted. But something about her ethic didn't fit with Olesk and his crew. She wasn't ruthless. She'd been against using a gun in San Francisco. He couldn't hold Marcos's death against her because she was new. But he didn't know what side she'd be on when he decided to destroy Olesk and his drivers.

Chapter Three

Stephanie woke with a gun in her hand. Several other noises had pulled her from a thin sleep, but the footsteps down the hallway had her fully aware and gripping her automatic. The metal was cold, the chill extending all the way into her bones. This was the world she was in now. Any second she might have to make the choice to pull the trigger.

The footsteps took a turn into the bathroom and she soon heard water running. Her watch told her it was after eight o'clock. Not nearly enough sleep, but her own discomfort couldn't matter until after this job was over.

She set her gun down and quickly changed into a fresh set of clothes before repacking her bag, including her pistol, and arranging herself for the day. The chair she'd wedged under the door handle remained in place; no one had tried to get in. She removed the chair and stepped into the empty hallway.

A second later, Arash opened the bathroom door. Water glistened in his dark hair, which had been released from its short ponytail to brush about his shoulders. He wore a tank top, revealing well-muscled arms and dusky skin. The flush of heat over her chest at seeing him this exposed proved that her body was still operational with little sleep. But she kept her face neutral and said only, "Morning."

He ran his hands through his hair, showing off the muscles of his shoulders. When she could see his face again, he was wearing a small, pained grin. "Why you gotta hurt me like that?" His voice was low and gravelly. Straight out of the bedroom.

She cleared her throat to erase the image of his piercing eyes glowing in the early dawn, his body surrounded by a tousled bed. "The truth hurts."

With a groaning laugh, he stepped out of the bathroom doorway and ambled toward his room. "What're the chances there's coffee around here?"

Ellie descended the stairs at the end of the hall with an answer. "Take the car in the garage." She tossed him a set of keys. "Keep your kit with you. Be ready to jump." She breezed past Arash and Stephanie without another word and disappeared out the front door of the house. An engine revved outside, then drove off. The house was quiet.

Stephanie was alone with Arash. "Two minutes," she told him, then closed the bathroom door. She emerged within her time frame to find him in the kitchen, fully dressed in his clothes from yesterday, nudging boxes of breakfast cereal on the counter. He still wore his hair down, making him seem more accessible and less like the man she saw running from a crime scene the night before.

"I'm driving." He dangled the car keys.

They went into the garage to find the Mercedes already gone. Her sense of loss was quickly swept away with the idea that the car had died a hero, getting her into Olesk's gang. Arash didn't seem to have any lingering feelings about it and climbed into the low sport-tuned import that remained in the garage. She tossed her bag into the back seat and climbed in next to him.

His hands hovered over the steering wheel and shifter for a moment. She understood this moment of assessing a vehicle before entering into a relationship with it. The car was modified and bare-bones. Racing seats and analog gauges. It didn't even have floor mats. But when Arash turned the engine over, she could feel the power in the quick growl. She hit the garage door opener on the visor, letting daylight in. Arash put the car in Reverse and eased out.

"How is it?" She closed the garage once they were clear.

"It's good." He didn't sound convinced. "But I could make it better." Throwing it in First, he sped them away from the house. "Find us some breakfast, and a mall. I need clothes." From the way he was squinting, he needed sunglasses, too.

She put on her own sunglasses and pulled out her phone to search for their next stop. Again, the urge to contact the others at Frontier Justice made her pause before switching to the navigation. But she was still far from being in a safe space. She knew the whole internal debate didn't last long enough for Arash to see her hesitation. He drove without comment as she directed them toward a mall.

Lack of sleep put a frothy edge around the bright, cool day. Things grew more ordinary when they parked and walked to the chain coffee shop on the perimeter of the mall. The morning crowd was still in full effect, restraining Stephanie and Arash's conversation to the bare minimum. They certainly couldn't compare notes about their first night in the midst of a criminal gang.

She ate and felt more human with each sip of her latte. Arash leaned his elbows on the table, both hands around his cup of coffee. He glanced surreptitiously at the others around them before asking, "What do you normally drive?"

The unexpected question made her shiver, as if an intimate barrier had been crossed. "'74 Datsun 260Z." No way would she have pretended to steal that one for Olesk.

He sat back and assessed her with surprise. And there was a hint of sadness in his eyes that blinked away before she could fully explore it. He mouthed a couple of words, then finally said, "You're hot."

"Changed the timing and compression ratio for more

horses." She adjusted the hang of her bob along her cheek. "Got the suspension low and tight, just how I like it."

He moaned sensuously, drawing a couple of looks. After licking his lips, he ventured, "Color?"

"Brick red. Matte."

"Hell, yes." He thumped the side of his fist on the table-top. A growing sexual energy in him caught her up. Breath ran hot in her and an effervescent tingle spiked her fingers and toes. And in a moment it was gone. Arash's face frosted over and he focused back on his cup of coffee. "I'd like to see it sometime."

She leaned forward and whispered, "Just don't steal it." Part of her missed the brief carnal connection they'd shared, but she knew it was for the best to keep this kind of contact shut down.

"No promises." He stood and nodded toward the door. She moved with him and they were soon back in the bright, cold sun. They'd only walked a couple dozen yards from the coffee shop when a car started up nearby and Arash froze.

His sudden reaction sent her into high alert. Electric charges shot through her legs, ready to move. She'd left her pistol in her bag in the car, knowing they were in too populated an area to carry it, but she did have a switch-blade in her pocket. "What is it?" she hissed, looking about for the threat.

"Can you hear it? Car trouble." He motioned her toward the idling, twenty-year-old sedan in a nearby parking spot and approached the driver with a greeting wave. A Latina woman dressed for an office job sat in the front seat, eyeing him cautiously. He pulled up at a nonthreatening distance and pointed at the front of the car. "I'm not trying to sell you anything. I just heard a little problem."

The driver rolled her window down, her gaze switching

between Arash and Stephanie. "I'm on my way to work and I don't have time…"

Arash kept his hands open and nodded. "I want to get you to work. No BS. If you could just rev the engine for a second."

The woman kept her hand on the shifter, ready to throw it into Drive and run, but did give the engine some gas while idling. Arash cocked his head, then nodded again. He maintained his distance and turned to Stephanie. "Do you hear it?"

She listened to the revving motor and found nothing out of the ordinary for a car of that age and make. But when the driver released the gas and brought it back to idle, a faint metallic double knock caught Stephanie's attention. "I think I got it."

Arash turned his attention back to the driver. "So there's a sound, a double knock, that goes away when you rev, but I hear it in your idle. Get your ride to a mechanic you trust and tell them that you might have a bad piston pin. They'll track it down. Take care of it soon, before it turns into big trouble."

The woman revved the engine again, squinting and concentrating when she brought it back to idle. Stephanie picked up the double knock again, but couldn't tell if the driver detected the sound. The driver seemed less skeptical and warmed with a small smile. "Thanks. I'll get it looked at." She put her car in Drive and headed out of the parking lot, waving out the window before she turned onto the boulevard.

Once she was gone, Arash continued his walk across the parking lot toward the mall. Stephanie strode with him, studying his face out of the corner of her eye, trying to find the motivation for what he just did. Instead of looking smug, or downright cocky, his expression was neutral. "You've got a good ear," she told him.

He stuffed his hands into the pockets of his jacket. In the light of day she saw that it was a simple black work jacket, heavy cotton with a corduroy collar. "Been living next to engines long enough."

"But you've got a soft heart." She couldn't puzzle him out at all.

"Not when it comes to business." His eyes hardened. He tipped his head in the direction where the woman had driven off. "I wasn't going to make any money off that ride. Wasn't going to fix it, steal it, part it out, joyride it or use it in a getaway. She was just trying to get to work, and I know a lot of people like that."

Sure, that sounded on the level, but did he know that by taking the gig with Olesk, Arash would be running boys and girls for some of the worst criminals in the country? Those people were just trying to live their lives, as well. Stephanie's chest tightened thinking about them. Before that anger took her over and she railed at Arash, she asked simply, "So what's your ride?"

"Mazda RX-7 Turbo II, '89."

"I can see that." He would fit well into the low-slung sports car, and there were plenty of opportunities to tune the ride into a well-handling street rocket. "White, with a turquoise roof?" It was from the '80s, after all.

He chuckled. "Matte black, completely murdered out." A hint of warmth cracked through his stony face. "That car…it's what my parents would've driven if they'd had any money once they'd settled in the States after getting out of Iran in the late '70s."

She kept reminding herself to hate him, or at least that she couldn't trust him, but hearing his softer tone when talking about his parents, or seeing the way he'd gone out of his way with the woman in the parking lot, Stephanie started to recognize that her job seeking justice was going to be way more complicated than she'd anticipated.

ARASH CURSED HIMSELF for helping the woman in the parking lot. He couldn't make any more mistakes like that. Not while Stephanie or anyone else from Olesk's gang was watching. She'd said he had a soft heart. Usually, he'd take that as a compliment, especially after all he'd seen growing up in the city. But a conscience had killed Marcos, and Arash had to stay alive to get revenge.

He hadn't been able to read Stephanie when she called him out. She wasn't directly looking down on him, or complimenting him, either. Her conscience remained a mystery. Under different circumstances, he'd try to trace her wiring, find out more of who she was. If this was just a simple road-trip fling, it would be different between them. So far there hadn't been much friction. Neither was trying to pull too much leverage over the other.

As they walked past the sliding glass doors to the mall, he wanted to reach out and take her hand. Maybe they could rush away from Olesk and this mess together. Or he could convince her to run while she still had the chance. Then he could find her once it was all over. He kept his hands in his pockets. The urge was impossible. She'd wanted to join up with Olesk. How the hell could he convince her to break that? One wrong word to her and she'd go to Olesk, putting a target on Arash's back. The only chance he had was to surprise the gang when they were all in one place. The big gig Olesk mentioned. He hated to think that he'd have to take Stephanie down, as well.

The morning people at the mall went about their business, wrangling kids, hurrying for last-minute items or strolling aimlessly like they had all the time in the world. None of them looked at Arash and Stephanie as if they were criminals. He navigated through the ordinary world, very much outside of it.

"Department store." Stephanie pointed to a multilevel store that anchored one side of the mall. "That should set you up, and I need some things, as well." She cruised forward, like she was completely comfortable in her skin.

While he was edged with bands of tension around his joints. Helping the woman in the parking lot was a lousy attempt to collect karma, and it hadn't offset that he was a bad guy again. It didn't matter if he had the best intentions. For the first time since running with burglars and car thieves in high school, he was part of a bad crew about to do bad things.

Stephanie stopped walking and stared at him as if waiting. He blinked at her and she spoke slowly. "Menswear." She moved her gaze deliberately to a sign off to their right. "That coffee hasn't kicked in?"

"Gonna need a gallon." Not true. He was fully awake, mind buzzing between guilt and revenge.

"Rally," she said. "Olesk could text any second and we have to be ready to burn."

"I'm on." He rolled his shoulders to move his blood.

"Do you need me to wait outside the dressing room?" she sassed.

"You can help me decide between boxers or briefs." He was a breath away from inviting her into the dressing room and testing how well they really balanced.

She took her time looking him up and down, giving him the sensation of cool river water running along his body. A shiver shook him and he was left thirsty for more. She finally gazed into his eyes and blinked slowly. "Split the difference. Boxer briefs." And she was gone, before he could answer or see if there was really a hint of heat in her eyes. She cruised easily toward the up escalator. He stared too long and she knew it, waving without turning around.

He turned and walked toward menswear. If she was watching from the escalator, he didn't give her anything except a casual strut. But inside, he stormed. He barely paid attention to the clothes he was grabbing. T-shirts, spare pair of jeans, sweatshirts, all of them dark colors. It didn't take long for his arm to be full, making his search through the socks and underwear more awkward than it should have been. Stephanie had called his bluff and identified his preferred underwear choice. No doubt she'd gloat if she saw the packages of boxer briefs on top of the rest of his pile of clothes.

A division of the menswear area had sport clothes and shoes, where he picked up a backpack to contain everything. In his normal life, he'd have been watching the price tags closer, but he had an envelope full of dirty cash in his jacket and wouldn't miss it once it was gone.

Arash peeled some hundred-dollar bills out of the envelope and pocketed them before walking his clothes to the cashiers at the front of the store. The young black man manning his station was cheerful and bored. They went through the requisite small talk, Arash saying he didn't need a bag because of the backpack. The cashier didn't blink when Arash handed over the crisp cash to pay, then took his change.

While Arash was stuffing his new clothes into the backpack, he could see out the front windows of the department store and into the mall. On the floor above him, Stephanie walked out the doors of a cell phone carrier and disappeared up the walkway. She wasn't moving too fast or looking over her shoulder, but it was still sketchy. He packed faster and hurried out of the department store with a thanks to the cashier.

When he hit the walkway in the mall, Stephanie was nowhere in sight. He got up to the second floor via a flight of stairs, trying to figure out all the justifications that she could've been at that store after not mentioning it before. And if she was doing something that wasn't in the best interest of Olesk and the gang, would Arash tell them? The convolutions knotted around him.

"Did you get your tighty-whities?" Stephanie's voice unfurled behind him.

He spun with surprise, unable to see how the hell she got there without him seeing her. He gathered his composure as quickly as possible. "Decided to go commando." That got a little laugh out of her and the convolutions complicated into a deadlier web. He pointed at the black bag she always carried and looked in her face, not at the cell phone store behind her. "Get what you needed?"

"I did," she said more cheerfully than he expected. "I'd forgotten a phone charger." She opened her bag and showed a DC charger branded with the store name she'd left a few moments ago.

A clean alibi, but maybe too deliberate. "Seems like something a planner like you would've thought of." He kept the tone casual.

"Not for the car." She started walking toward the exit of the mall and he strode next to her. "Didn't know we'd be on the move this much."

"Good point." He hadn't even thought to bring along a wall charger.

"Don't worry—it'll charge two phones at once."

"You do think of everything." But he wasn't entirely convinced she wasn't sketchy. But then again, in the light of day, they were both crooks.

"Even had some time to buy some jewelry." She held up her hand to show that two of the fingers were encircled with fine gold bands. One formed an X, the other crisscrossed, like the tracks of a planet orbiting her. "And…" Her hand disappeared into her bag before he stared at it too long. "I found something for you." She produced a box containing a burly sport watch.

He took it as she offered it, but he didn't open the box. The watch was definitely his style. But he couldn't figure out what the endgame was for her. Part of him burst with a small flare of pleasure at her gesture. "I can't take this."

"It's not from me," she explained, holding out her palm in refusal to take it back. "It's from the woman with the faulty piston pin." A warmer light shined in her eyes, pulling him closer to her. "I know you didn't do it to get paid." Neither spoke for a moment.

"Thanks." He opened the box and put the watch on his wrist.

Stephanie backed off a bit. He wanted to reach for the connection again, but he didn't know if he could trust it. She fixed the edges of her hair. "Besides, Olesk has us on a tight schedule. I can't have you driving and checking the time on your phone."

"Always planning."

"Exactly." She reached into her bag again and produced a pair of black sunglasses, which she held toward him.

He backed away, shaking his head. "But I'm all out of good deeds." Yes, he didn't have any sunglasses and she took the time to notice. Any pleasure in her thoughtfulness was overshadowed by the complex and deadly maze he found himself walking blindly within.

"These are from me." She stepped to him, sunglasses still extended. "If I'm riding shotgun, I can't have my driver squinting into the sun." Her face was serious, without a wry smile or irony in her voice.

The labyrinth around him shifted and spun. He'd steeled himself with heartless resolve for this journey of revenge and hadn't expected to find any good here. But Stephanie wasn't good. He had to keep reminding himself that to combat the lightness in his chest she could evoke with the smallest gesture.

"I'm your driver." He took the sunglasses.

For a moment, they seemed exposed. He was free from the lies and the crime and faced her as a man facing a woman. She stared back at him boldly, without artifice. And there was a heat in her eyes, a reflection of the attraction that pulled him closer to her. Her lips parted with a breath, and he wanted so much to know what she tasted like. What she would feel like slammed against him.

Then the moment was gone. She stepped back and pulled her buzzing phone from her back pocket. "Olesk," she explained, a slight huskiness in her voice. She cleared her throat and erased the warmth in her eyes. "We're on the move. He says to get a full tank of gas and head east. More instructions to follow."

The labyrinth erupted all around Arash again. He strode with Stephanie into the parking lot, slipping his sunglasses on. "I'm your driver." And he couldn't let himself feel anything anymore because every turn ahead was deadly.

Chapter Four

Stephanie spun one of the new rings around her finger. She slowed her breath and tried to keep the building tension from breaking her apart. Arash pumped gas into the compact racer while she sat in the passenger seat. Her cell phone rested on her thigh, ready for the next move. She couldn't read Arash's eyes behind the dark sunglasses she'd bought for him, but she could see his jaw was clenched. Both of them knew something was coming.

Whatever she was about to rush into, she had a sliver of confidence now that Frontier Justice had been updated on her situation. It had been a mad rush to get through the department store, then up to the cell phone place before Arash had made his way through his shopping. Luckily the young white woman set up the contract-free phone quickly, allowing Stephanie the time to call in her "stolen" car to her insurance company for the sake of verisimilitude in case Olesk was looking hard in that direction.

Texting Ty and the others from Frontier Justice her flood of information while standing in a service hallway of the mall had tested all her composure. She was sure some words were jumbled or autocorrected improperly, but she had to get everything out before sending one last message: This phone is burned. She'd pulled the battery and SIM card out, scraped the SIM card against the wall until it was unusable, then threw it all out in a trash can behind Arash before he'd spotted her.

But the man was sharp. As soon as he'd turned to her with suspicion in his eyes, she'd known he'd seen her at the phone store. She'd had all the excuses lined up, but still he'd remained cagey. Neither of them was on solid footing.

Especially once she'd given him the gifts. What had started as an honest want to repay him for helping the woman in the parking lot, and Stephanie's selfish need to have her driver not wrapping their car around a power pole because the sun was in his eyes, turned too damn intimate too quickly. His appreciation for the gesture gave her way more of a thrill than she'd expected.

It had felt like they'd been speeding without brakes toward each other. Sometimes she longed for a reckless crash. This one, though, could have deadly consequences. Olesk's text had come at just the right time.

Arash finished fueling the car and leaned into the open driver's-side window. "Any word?"

She checked her phone, even though she'd looked at it two seconds ago. "Nothing."

"Food allergies?"

"No, but I hate coconut."

"What a shame." He sauntered to the gas station convenience store, shaking his head the whole way.

Two seconds later her phone buzzed. Olesk texted them an intersection and a time frame. She was about to slide over into the driver's seat when Arash returned, faster than he'd left. He tossed two bottles of water and a handful of candy bars into the back seat and rushed behind the wheel. The car was already out of the gas station and onto the street by the time he asked, "Where to?"

She read him the directions from the map, then checked the time. "Seven minutes."

"I saw you going for the driver's seat, but I couldn't let

you have all the fun." His grin was wilder than his driving through the flow of traffic. She knew it wouldn't take much for him to turn it loose. He pulled his phone from his jacket and handed it over to her. "Can you throw this on the charger?"

She hooked him up, then directed him through the next intersection. Their destination was close and they were running early for a change. Pride at a job well done was quickly tempered by the knowledge that she was aiding criminals. The same went for the rush she felt from the coordination between her and Arash. It didn't matter who was driving and who was shotgun; they handled their jobs and kept each other moving. Her brief elation dived quickly into a sense of loss for what could've been in a very different world.

As soon as he hit a straightaway, Arash pulled a hair band from his pocket and swept his hair back into that small ponytail, fully revealing his sharp features. "Good call on the sunglasses." He looked over to her for a second before turning his attention back to the road.

"They look fly." She'd considered a couple frames before settling on these and was rewarded by him looking sexy and severe.

"You have good taste." He shook his wrist to flash the watch. A perfect fit.

"Except when it comes to men." If she really had good taste, she wouldn't be feeling small electric thrills raining up through her as she looked over this car-thief criminal with his rough hands all over the steering wheel and shifter.

Instead of shutting him down like she'd hoped, it evoked a quick laugh and an even wilder smile. When he stood harder on the gas, making the engine moan, the bastard knew she couldn't look away.

She reminded herself of everything at stake, cooled herself and flattened her voice. "After the next right is our intersection. We're one minute early. Circle until I hear the next move."

"Understood." Arash must've known better than to push her any further and matched the businesslike tone.

Her phone buzzed. She read, "'Run interference for white cube van with Nevada plates. Draw any cops off.'"

"I've got eyes on the truck." He tipped his head to their left, where a medium-sized cargo truck trundled out of a storage-facility parking lot.

"You know them?" She didn't recognize the driver or the man riding shotgun.

"No, but there's Olesk and Ellie." They were in a sport-tuned Subaru that was clearly straining against its muscle as it cruised half a block behind the truck. Olesk drove and Ellie rode passenger with a cell phone in her hand. She acknowledged Arash and Stephanie with a brief nod before swiveling her gaze to take in the area.

Stephanie did the same. "If they need us for interference, then they know someone's onto this move." There'd been a couple of local PD blips regarding Olesk's gang in the Frontier Justice control center she'd helped install in Mariana's farmhouse. It pulled radio signals, internet leads and poached cell phone conversations from law enforcement and back-channel sources in an attempt to track the Seventh Syndicate and other organizations that were attacking anyone who couldn't defend themselves. Fitting that the hub of all this information was the home where Frontier Justice had started over a hundred years ago.

And Stephanie knew that farmhouse was still in good hands. Mariana was the perfect fit for Ty, both determined as hell. Their strong wills extended out to their unwavering care for the other, something Stephanie knew was a rarity in this world.

"Unmarked car at seven o'clock." Arash shifted his vision from the side mirror to the road ahead. Stephanie snapped out of her thoughts and spun to check behind them. The dark brown car had state-exempt plates and a nearly invisible flasher bar in front of the visors.

"He's driving like he means it." The police car slipped past Olesk and Ellie, on the hunt. Instead of relief arriving with the police, Stephanie's pulse kicked faster. Olesk and the STR couldn't get busted before she'd pierced all the way to the Seventh. "Run him off."

"Olesk has him." Arash held back amid the normal traffic. The Subaru separated out and sped forward. After passing the unmarked car, Olesk swerved hard in front of it and raced up a side street. The police car couldn't resist the bait. The light bar strobed on and its tires chirped before propelling it after the Subaru. "No discipline. Those cops should've stayed on their mark."

"Whose side are you on?" she quipped, hoping no one would ever ask her that question.

"Cash money." His mouth thinned. She locked a snapshot of the moment in her memory, to be pulled out every time she felt herself being drawn toward this man.

The cube van continued up the wide boulevard, and she started to predict the route. "They're heading for the highway." A police patrol car pulled quickly onto the street. "Cruiser." There was no sign of Olesk or the unmarked car.

"On it." Arash broke out of the normal flow of traffic but held two car lengths back from the police car. She surged forward in her seat and put her foot down like she had her own gas pedal. He shook his head. "We've got to know what they know. If they're onto the truck, it doesn't matter how many distractions we throw at them. Helicopters, roadblocks, highway patrol will come down hard."

She knew he was right. Whatever intel the police were acting off must've been vague, because the patrol car seemed to be searching rather than following the truck directly. Even when it had a free lane to slide up behind the truck, it held back, and other cars filled in the space. "They're hunting blind."

Arash rolled his shoulders and snugged himself into the racing seat. "Let's give them something to chase." He downshifted and the car lurched forward with power, then it sped when he threw it into the next gear. Instead of sweeping past the patrol car, Arash steered off the boulevard and across the corner of a strip mall parking lot.

"Looks like you suffer from premature acceleration." She watched in the side-view mirror as the police car disappeared up the boulevard.

Arash laughed and slowed the car. "He saw us," he reassured her. "Didn't want to make it look like we were deliberately distracting him from the real target."

"That was Olesk's move."

"Exactly." He pointed in the rearview mirror and she turned to see the patrol car coming after them along the residential street. "Too cocky." He stepped on the gas. The cops didn't hesitate to give chase and they were soon blasting past parked cars and winter-bare London plane trees.

It seemed like the police would catch up to them. Blue-and-red flashing lights were close enough to color the interior of Stephanie and Arash's car. A voice came over the loudspeaker between siren blasts. "Stop the car. Stop the car and pull to the right." Arash was only in third gear. "Stop immediately."

Arash hung back another second, then stepped on the gas. The car shot forward, leaving the police voice a jumble behind them. The patrol car sped to catch up, but its engine could already be heard straining. She spun to watch the police, seeing the passenger on the radio. "Backup will be incoming."

"Anyone who wants to get embarrassed is welcome to show up to this party." Arash downshifted around a corner and put a full block between them and the pursuing police.

"You got your wish." They pulled back onto the main boulevard just as two more marked police cars hurried into the area. The cops were quick to turn on their sirens and clear a path to Stephanie and Arash.

"Any sign of the truck?" Arash upped their speed but maintained a calm approach that never felt reckless.

She searched over the street and saw they were right by an on-ramp for the highway. "No truck. They must've hit the highway."

"What the hell's our next move?" Arash bared his teeth as he made another hard turn off the boulevard and into another neighborhood. The police had to stack one in front of the other, limiting their tactical maneuvers.

Stephanie looked over the map on her phone for any areas where they could lose this kind of pursuit. "Train tracks four blocks ahead and to the left might lead to a depot or warehouses we could lose these rollers in." Her phone buzzed in her hand. "Text from Olesk. They lost their tail. We've got to do the same and hit the highway east. Clock's ticking before the police scramble a chopper."

Arash muscled the car around another hard turn, gritting out, "You know, this would go a lot better if that freaking mastermind let us in on the plan beforehand."

"Don't go right," she called out after looking at the map. "Cul-de-sac."

"I can work with that." He veered right and slowed enough for the police cars to catch up.

"I'd have tried a different approach." She tensed in her seat and braced her hand on the door panel.

"We can't agree on everything." He sped forward again, then yanked up on the emergency brake and jammed the steering wheel to one side. Tires screamed as the car's rear swung an arc in the cul-de-sac to bring them one hundred eighty degrees around. Once they were facing the oncoming police cars, Arash released the brake and hit the gas. "That would be boring."

The cops knew better than to play chicken and slammed on their brakes. The two cars staggered, blocking the way out. Arash charged forward, a small smile on his lips. She clenched her jaw and wrapped her fist around the handle above the side window. A hard impact could come any second. They were going fast enough to kill. At the last second, Arash swung the car off the road and into a driveway to the right. They bounced onto the sidewalk and paralleled the street for a second, sending the police cars to scramble into reverse.

Arash turned hard again, taking them over the curb and crossing onto the street between the two cop cars. One car slammed to a stop. The other swerved and fishtailed before jamming its rear into a parked car, blocking the first car from the action. Arash drove back off the street and onto the opposite sidewalk, which was clear enough to get them completely away from the cul-de-sac.

They cruised back onto a normal road, free from police. The engine calmed, but her heart still pounded. She gathered her breath and navigated Arash to the freeway on-ramp. He let out a long sigh once they were moving with the flow. But when they both spotted a highway patrol car stalking about a quarter mile ahead, the atmosphere tightened again in the car.

"Use that semi for rolling cover." She pointed to a truck hauling a tall load of cargo. Arash nodded and eased the car alongside, between them and the highway patrol.

He kept pace with the truck, even though they had plenty of lane to pass and speed ahead. He grumbled, "Goes against everything I know about driving next to trucks."

"I feel you." She always gave the rigs a large halo of space. "But it's working." From her perspective, there was no sign of the highway patrol, meaning they must be parallel with them. "I think we're good to get up front." Arash added speed and merged into the semi's lane. She checked all around and couldn't see the police, so they couldn't see them.

After two miles of staying within cautious cover of the truck, Arash moved into the faster flow of traffic. She stayed alert for highway patrol, but allowed her body to calm in waves. Her legs ached as she drew her feet back from being braced hard on the floor. The slowing of her heartbeat allowed for a new elation to take over through her limbs. Damn it. It was like good sex.

Arash leaned more casually in his seat, one hand on the steering wheel, jaw relaxed and mouth less severe. She stared at the cords of his neck too long, wondering if she'd be able to feel his pulse match hers. He kept his face forward and put out a fist to her. "Job well done." But there was a minor note in his voice, barely detectable.

"I guess you can drive." She bumped his fist with hers.

He sneered a small smile. "Ask those cops." Through his bravado was that dark thread. She tried to follow it, but the trail deeper into him dissolved before she could grab hold. *For the best*, she convinced herself. *Keep him at a distance.* But she still wanted to know.

A text came through on her phone. "Olesk," she reported. "Next stop—Reno."

Miles farther away from any safety. Deeper into the danger. Exactly where she needed to be going. Though, traveling there with Arash at her side shook her compass. She knew she would not waver in helping the victims in need, but she now questioned who she would have to become to get this mission accomplished, and how far her hunger for Arash would take her.

Chapter Five

"It's beautiful." But he didn't feel it. Driving through the mountains like this, with a crisp blue sky, a noon sun and a tailwind pushing him forward, should've made Arash breathe easier. He'd taken this route before, just for the sake of the strip of asphalt among the trees, with the Truckee River flashing below in the cold sunlight. This trip, the threat of danger around every turn robbed him of his peace.

"It is." Stephanie stared out the window, her eyes invisible behind stylish aviator sunglasses. All the times he'd driven this road to escape the city for a day or two, he'd never had a passenger. If he wasn't driving one of Olesk's cars, if they hadn't just evaded the police during a job for the STR, if Stephanie wasn't part of that same gang, he'd allow himself to enjoy this with her.

They'd covered many of the miles in alert silence. Highway patrol had been quiet, and there'd been no more texts from Olesk with last-second directives to chase down. Drive-through food would've slowed them down too much, so he ate his candy bars and drank his water just to keep his mood from crashing.

"You know where you're going." Stephanie's gaze remained on the scenery.

"I know the road." But he had no idea what his final destination would look like. If he'd had the chance, he could've taken Marcos out here, maybe after the first snow so they could see there was more to the world than the underside of a Chevy or the engine bay of a Honda. Marcos would never see these mountains, even though it was he who got Arash onto the highway for this trip.

"Running goods across the lines?" she asked dryly.

The question stabbed through his ribs and held with cold barbs. She thought he was a crook. But why wouldn't she? "I only work in Cali. I'm not on the Feds' radar." Half-truths. His criminal days had ended before his eighteenth birthday. The few things he'd been caught for prior to that had been sealed. And why should he care what she thought of him? She was a crook, too. "Am I riding next to someone with active warrants?"

"Do you think I ever get caught?" She turned to him and smiled.

"Never." He shook his head.

Her attention shifted back to the window. "So how do you know this highway?"

"I come out here to test handling and suspension."

"Long way from the city."

"That's the point." Someday he might be able to afford one of the lodges or hotels in the mountains, instead of finding one of the cheaper rooms down in Reno.

"I've done it on a motorcycle." She turned forward and tilted her head to match a wide curve.

"Sexy." He wished he could stop flirting with her, but the two of them seemed to flow so easily. Imagining her in the seat behind him as he drove a motorcycle, wrapped around him, the insides of her thighs against his hips, thinned the air more than the altitude around them.

"The *route*." She shot him a frown. "I've done the *route* on a motorcycle. SF to Tahoe, I-80."

"I know what you meant." He stared at the road ahead instead of her black-jean-clad legs stretched out in front of her. "And it's still sexy."

"I could be married." She held up her left hand, though it had no ring on the ring finger. "What would my wife think about you saying that?"

He slowed the car as they passed a small mountain town. "I don't tread on someone else's territory. Tell her I'm sorry and from now on you and I are going to stick to talking about the weather and onboard diagnostic codes for troubleshooting air/fuel efficiency."

"Now that's sexy."

"Damn it." Sometimes she could be so dry that he had no idea if she was joking or not. "What's your wife going to say?"

She crossed her arms. "I'm not married." Hearing that lit more of a thrill in him than he wanted. "You?" she asked.

"I'm too greasy for that." He'd just gotten into a steady groove wrenching at a new garage, and he was thinking his social life might open up when Marcos hit his rough patch. There'd been no time for dating. After Marcos's death, it took weeks for Arash to develop any stomach for company.

"Slippery while all the girls are trying to catch you." She turned one of the new rings around her finger.

"You've seen me drive a getaway." Of course the first woman he felt attracted to was part of the whole problem he was messed up with.

She chuckled. "That's how you leave all your dates in the morning. Redlining and drifting around corners."

"Morning?" he scoffed. "I can't have them reading my license plate."

The road curved and brought a stand of jagged mountains into view. Winter had barely begun, yet snow dusted some ridges to create stark contrasts between dark and light. He and Stephanie fell silent. The mountains were so much larger than his troubles. They were timeless, unlike his thirst for revenge, which would be extinguished if he died. He felt like he was hurtling toward all their sharp edges.

The quiet continued through the high pass. When the road started the descent toward Reno, Stephanie spoke. "We've got to ditch this car."

"Feel like a target." A bigger city meant more police presence. They had no idea how wide the description of the car had gone. "And I could use a hot meal."

"I know a good pizza in Tahoe City."

"What do you know in Reno?"

"Nothing." She swiped through her phone.

"I've had a couple decent burgers out here." But it was a big town, and their destination could be miles from anywhere he knew. "No address from Olesk yet?"

"You know how he likes to play it." She released a frustrated breath.

"It's almost like he doesn't want us in the STR." Aggravation dug into him like a headache, shortening his patience.

"Just making us jump through hoops to prove ourselves." She waved her hand dismissively and smoothed herself to seem untouched by Olesk's antics.

Arash steered with tighter fists. "It's not professional. And I'm a professional." People knew his name in the garages of San Francisco and Oakland. He worked hard and was respected. That reputation might be wrecked now that he'd taken time away from his current shop to chase Olesk's blood. Arash had known as soon as he'd answered the man's first text that there was probably no going back. Ever.

The mountains loomed in the rearview mirror like a passing storm, soon replaced by the buildings of Reno. The little calm that had come with the natural surroundings was erased by the growing anxiety of being in the city. More eyes watched them. Traffic swirled. Security cameras hung high on power poles. The police patrolled.

A cold, inhospitable wind swept over it all. Arash stayed on the highway, where he had the best visibility, though if trouble did come for them, his evasive options were limited. Stephanie sat up straighter, her phone clutched in her hand and her awareness constantly swiveling to take in the surroundings.

"If we don't hear anything, I'll pass through west to east, then double back." He calculated what he knew of the layout.

"Sounds good." Her voice was tight. "I've been looking over local news between Sacramento and here but haven't found anything about any police chases or busts."

Frustration ground his nerves down. Was this it? Olesk got what he needed from Arash and now cut him off? But Arash wouldn't let it end that way. He nearly swerved into another lane when Stephanie's phone buzzed. She sighed with relief and reported, "Olesk. Freaking finally." She read out an address he didn't recognize, then started navigating them into the northeast fringe of the city.

The highway only took them so far. They exited to a two-lane road that slipped quickly through suburbs and into less populated areas. Fewer services were seen and the territory seemed appropriate for homesteaders and apocalyptic preppers. There wasn't much blood flowing to this part of town. The houses that could be seen from the road were set back behind expansive dirt lots, complete with large propane tanks, oversize television antennae and opaque plastic-covered greenhouses.

"They'd better have lunch." Stephanie watched it all with an impassive face.

Food was the last thing on his mind. He was on high alert, trying to play those eight moves ahead. Anger and frustration swirled through him, tightening his neck and shoulders, and he didn't know if he should work through them or let them fly.

The properties on the side of the road spread out farther. Acres separated the mailboxes and the transitions in the types of fences. "Less than a mile." Stephanie watched her phone. "On the right."

The next plot of land emerged and Arash turned up a long dirt lane toward a large stucco house. Cars and motorcycles collected in the curved front driveway, some of them looking fresh, others broken down. An RV was parked on the side of the house. Beyond it, he glimpsed two metal barns with closed doors. Skeletons of cars and trucks lay around those structures, as if they'd died before reaching an oasis.

Once Arash and Stephanie were within fifty yards of the house, two figures emerged from the front door. Olesk and Ellie walked down from the porch to the driveway, then over to the left of the house. Olesk motioned Arash forward and pointed toward the barns.

Stephanie gave them a wave and casually pulled her bag from the back seat and onto her lap. Arash sensed a flicker of extra tension in her. Did she have a gun in that bag? All he was armed with was a folding knife and a flashlight. If Olesk wanted them to disappear, this would be a perfect place to do it.

Rounding the house, Arash saw the white cargo truck from Sacramento parked next to one of the barns. Two men, one white, one Hispanic, he recognized from the cab of the cargo truck watched Arash's and Stephanie's approach, then went to the front of the barn and opened the doors.

The interior was a stark black rectangle of shadow compared to the bright day. Arash eased inside, his gut clenching and his awareness churning to take in any necessary details. The back wall of the barn was solid, but he might be able to break through it if he could get enough speed up in the car. There were high windows that had been painted over, if he had time to climb the metal shelving filled with shop tools and auto parts.

Arash brought the car to a stop and shared a quick look with Stephanie. He couldn't see her eyes behind her sunglasses, but he sensed her caution. He gave her a small nod and she returned it. Grabbing his backpack, he slid from the car and stood to face out of the barn. Stephanie did the same on the other side of the car.

Olesk, Ellie and the two other men silhouetted against the bright, sere landscape. Their hands hung at their sides, but if any of them made a move, Arash was ready to charge across the dirt floor. The chances of taking the gang down on their own territory were less than zero. He would die trying.

"There's food in the house." Olesk's casual, welcoming tone ripped at Arash's last nerve.

"Food?" Arash stalked forward. The two men he didn't know instantly puffed up for a fight. The Hispanic man was about his size; the white guy next to him, taller and leaner. If they didn't pull any weapons, he'd be happy to blow off his steam taking them on. He barked out at Olesk, "How about a map, or a plan, or some information so we're not hung out to dry with our asses on the line?"

Olesk cocked his head, relaxed. "You handled everything." The other men balled their fists.

"A split second away from getting burned." Arash ignored the other guys who glared at him and focused on Olesk. "You want me to do my job with less potential for disaster, I need more info as I go." Olesk just shrugged, making Arash wish the two men would make a play so he could put his fist into someone's face. "I come on here and deliver for you and you act like you don't trust me. You think I'm going to rat?" It was probably a bad idea to come after the boss of the gang like this, but Arash had his pride and standards to protect. And if he played too easily into

Olesk's game, it might bring about more suspicion than the hard moves he was putting on now.

"Does he speak for you?" Olesk shifted his unblinking gaze deeper into the barn, to Stephanie.

Stephanie's voice slid cool over Arash's shoulder. "I always speak for myself." He was glad she stood on her own. He didn't need her to back him up and he definitely wasn't going to drag her unwillingly into this conflict. She continued calmly, "Whether I'm driving or riding shotgun, knowledge is power." Her even footsteps approached until he was able to see her in his peripheral vision. There was as much poise in her body as her words. "You loop me in, I do a better job."

Ellie jutted her jaw and squinted with displeasure. Olesk kept it smooth and nodded. "Yeah, you got it. This one was a little tight and we were all scrambling." He spoke to both Stephanie and Arash. "It isn't always like that." He tipped his head toward the house. "Your cash is inside. Hope you like frozen pizza."

It wasn't a straight-up apology, but it was good enough. Arash pulled his backpack onto his shoulder. "As long as you've got an oven." He took a step to follow Olesk and Ellie, but the two men remained in their bar-fight posture in front of him. Ellie rolled her eyes.

Olesk huffed a small laugh. "Thom, Hector, meet Arash and Stephanie."

The white man nodded when Olesk had announced "Thom." This guy was a user. Restless, red-rimmed eyes. Arash had seen the same effects of crank on his friend before this gang had rubbed him out. Thom's dirty blond hair was greasy, and his lips always seemed to be moving, like he was just about to say something.

Hector, who looked to be in his twenties and appeared to spend most of his time either in the gym or working on his sweep of hair, reluctantly tipped his head. "What's up?" He took his time looking Stephanie up and down.

"You're welcome." She sauntered forward with a challenge.

That brought Thom's brow down, revealing wrinkles on the fortysomething-year-old man. "For what, honey?"

She hesitated for a split second, as if holding herself back, then answered, "For running those cops off your tail." With a bright smile, she stepped past Thom and Hector and into the sun.

Hector fired at her back, "In the car that we tuned."

Arash scoffed, "The car with too much lag in second gear and a turbo booster spraying oil." Thom's wild gaze landed back on Arash. "Didn't you smell it?"

Neither Thom nor Hector answered.

"I smelled it." Stephanie nodded her head.

A loud laugh barked from Olesk. He wagged a finger at Arash and Stephanie. "Yeah, you're STR. Definitely." After putting his arm around Ellie's hip, he headed to the house.

Thom and Hector deflated and fell into step. Arash and Stephanie moved along with them. Winter chill sliced into his neck above the collar of his jacket. It didn't matter how high the sun was, it couldn't chase this cold. Inside his chest, though, Arash was a furnace. Now that he was in with the gang, he would have to plot how to wipe them out. Somewhere on the highway, where he knew he was a better driver than any of them. Except maybe Stephanie. The last thing he wanted to do was to bring her down with the rest of them.

She shifted so she was walking next to Thom. Her smooth voice warned, "Call me *honey* one more time, and I take one of your kneecaps."

"Sure," Thom sneered.

She stopped walking and took off her sunglasses. He

turned and she stared him dead in the eye, challenging through her teeth, "Do it."

Her dare hung in the icy air. Arash and the others waited. Hector puffed up again. Olesk dropped his hand from Ellie's waist and the two of them watched intently. If Thom bit back, and Stephanie had to fight him and anyone else, Arash could get to Hector before he got to her. After a long three seconds, Thom blinked and chewed his tongue and didn't say anything. Stephanie put her sunglasses back on and breezed past him. Arash remained at her side, knowing that Hector and Thom stared hard from behind them.

He walked toward the house. Each step closer to payback. Along this path, Stephanie was the only one who'd shown him any trust. He'd just discovered that he was willing to throw down for her. But he couldn't rely on the same from Stephanie once his true intent was known. At that moment, there would be nowhere safe for him. And the connection he was beginning to savor with Stephanie would be dead.

Chapter Six

Stephanie stood in the cold heart of Olesk's crew and had to pretend that she belonged. Even if she could inform Frontier Justice of her location, it would take someone hours to arrive. Any trouble, she had to handle herself. Although it seemed from her confrontation with Thom that Arash had her back. He'd stood at the ready, hands flexed and face scowling. It had given her more of a flash of appreciative heat than she wanted to admit. But where would Arash's loyalty come down when the battle lines were finally drawn?

She ignored the question. The time frame stretched out beyond her knowledge and she could only deal with surviving the here and now until she had more information. At least Olesk was loosening up. He'd shown Arash and Stephanie their rooms on the second floor of the sprawling house, then they'd all reconvened in the white-tiled open kitchen.

The oven ticked and clanged as it worked on a frozen pizza for Arash and Stephanie. Her stomach was ready for it, but her taste buds were hoping for more savory satisfaction than the thin disc would provide. The house was warm, comfortable enough, but she kept her jacket on to obscure the pistol she'd holstered at the small of her back as soon as she'd had a second alone in her new room.

Thom and Hector sat at a small table tucked into a bay

window with a view of the dirt field and barns behind the house. Hector nursed a beer and Thom toyed with the condensation on a tall energy drink can as they murmured sporadically.

Arash stood on the opposite side of the dining area, with Olesk at a different window with the same view. They talked and pointed at various things in the back, but Stephanie didn't feel shut out. She'd already proven her worth, and when something important was on, they'd come to her.

She pulled off a bottle of sparkling water and leaned against the counter as Ellie rummaged through the refrigerator next to her. With a slam, Ellie closed the door and twisted the cap off a bottle of beer with that perpetual judgy look on her face. Like she was wringing someone's neck. Instead of skulking off to a dark corner in the barely decorated house like Stephanie expected her to do, Ellie sat back against the counter next to her and looked out of the kitchen and dining area.

She took a pull off her beer, then spoke low with her lips still near the bottle. "I wish you'd torn Thom a new one."

"I still might, depending on his manners." Stephanie checked her watch and saw there were still a few minutes left for the pizza.

Ellie smiled wistfully, then grew serious again. "Don't worry about the information flow. Just a bit of initiation." She toasted Stephanie's water with her beer. "I got to move that Merc you brought in. You definitely passed the test."

"Someone's going to miss that car." Part of her longed for the simplicity of taking that car along the coast down Highway 1 and through the Monterey Bay. Without danger, or pursuit. Or Arash confusing everything.

"*I* miss it after one drive." Ellie drained half of her beer. "He's legit?" She stared at Arash, who continued his conversation with Olesk.

"He doesn't play it safe." Which had turned out to be way too exciting. "But he gets the job done."

"That'll do." Ellie set her empty bottle on the counter and retrieved a fresh one from the fridge. "We drive hard, we get paid." She pulled a thick white envelope from her back pocket and handed it to Stephanie.

"Do you drive?" Stephanie thumbed over the stack of cash. All the blood money she collected from Olesk would go into making Frontier Justice stronger.

Ellie quirked her matte plum-colored lips into a wry smile. "Only on the left side of the road." She leaned off the counter and walked away to Arash and Olesk. Pulling another envelope from her pocket, she toasted Arash with her beer. He answered with a tip of his head and took the envelope from her.

"You didn't bring me a beer?" Olesk spoke a little too loudly and his voice echoed off the hard bare surfaces of the kitchen and dining room.

"Sorry, hon." Ellie took a long pull from her bottle, not breaking eye contact with him.

Arash ducked the interaction and walked toward the kitchen area while glancing down at the cash in the envelope. If the eight thousand dollars impressed him, he didn't show it. A shadow crossed his face for a moment, angry and dark. It was gone by the time he pocketed the money and reached Stephanie next to the stove. "How much longer on the pizza?"

"Does it matter?" She checked her watch.

"No." He opened the oven and used a kitchen towel to pull the tray out. "Need to eat hot food." Cheese bubbled and sauce spattered and it didn't look as bad as she'd made it out to be. He put it on top of the stove, shut the oven and collected two paper plates from a stack on the island. "You guys have a pizza cutter?"

Thom laughed. "We're not fancy like that."

"It's not fancy, it's a freaking pizza cutter." Arash tugged drawers open.

"Get a knife," Hector called out.

Stephanie turned the oven off and pulled a cheap serrated knife from a knife block on the counter. Arash stopped his search and squared up with her, gaze flicking between the blade and her face. He balanced on the balls of his feet like a fight was coming and the darkness glimmered in his eyes again. "You know how to use that."

"I can cook."

"That's not what I mean." He glanced at the knife block, his hands empty, but open and ready.

She laid the knife down on the counter. "Did some courier work in the city." Her father had never been so furious than when he'd learned that she'd convinced some of his runners to let her take over their routes collecting and delivering stacks of cash. "Didn't lose a single package." But her regular bank account had been frozen for two months and she'd had to rely on the online money market accounts she'd created for herself.

"No doubt." He took up the knife, segmented the pizza and slid the slices onto the paper plates. There were open seats at the table with Thom and Hector, but Arash and Stephanie leaned against the island to eat.

Ellie sauntered back into the kitchen, collected two beers from the fridge and returned to Olesk. He clinked his bottle against hers and spoke to the room. "The plan so far— Hector and Thom are starting the van makeovers with the goods we got out of Sactown." Stephanie chilled. Those vans were made for moving people. "Arash and Stephanie, you two break down the tuner that got you here."

"How far down?" Arash asked between bites.

"All the way." Olesk made a spiraling motion with his beer. "It's a donor now. Without a trace."

"Ready to get greasy with me?" Arash flicked her a look.

Her body responded to his wicked grin with a needy hunger, deep in her chest. It was impossible to shut down, no matter how much logic she threw at it.

Olesk sauntered through the dining area. "There are more local jobs coming, so settle in and don't worry about hopping too quickly. I'll let you know this time." He saluted with his beer. "As soon as the tuner's in parts and in boxes we'll throw Arash and Steph at the van project."

"Stephanie," she corrected him. Ellie smiled to herself.

"Stephanie." Olesk threw her name over his shoulder as he wandered into another part of the house with Ellie, probably one of the two living rooms with gigantic TVs.

Arash ate in silence. As soon as Stephanie took a bite of the warm food, she didn't care how it tasted and just knew she needed the sustenance. Hector finished his beer, laid it on its side and tapped Thom on the shoulder. They wordlessly agreed to head out and stood together. Hector pointed toward a side door out of the dining area. "There are disposable coveralls in the mudroom."

"All the tools are in the barn?" Stephanie asked.

"With power and a compressor." Hector nodded. "You two come find us if things get too complicated under the hood."

"Don't forget," Thom added with a watery smirk. "Righty tighty, lefty loosey."

Arash mocked a smile, but his eyes remained hard and cold. Deadly with the darkness she still hadn't figured out in him. Thom had no answer for the malice and hunched slightly as he exited to the rest of the house with Hector. Arash muttered, "Could break him like chicken bones."

"Not your favorite?" She'd eaten all she could of the pizza and threw the crusts in the trash.

"He's definitely not invited to my birthday party." Arash pulled away from the island.

Her laugh echoed louder than she expected through the

kitchen. The meanness in Arash's smile disappeared when he looked at her. The warmth tugged too strongly at her. She tried to cut it off and walked to the side door Hector had indicated. But she still felt Arash with her, even though he was a few strides behind her and hadn't pressed the moment any further.

Through the door was a mudroom with high cabinets over a washer and dryer, along with a utility sink draped with rags. Several bottles of bleach stood under the sink. The whole area was so sterile she knew it had been used to clean up very illegal messes. Arash's face drained of any warmth, going blank as he opened the cabinets. He pulled down two pairs of Tyvek coveralls and handed one to Stephanie before opening a heavier door to the outside.

Cold air swept in on a dry breeze, and she didn't know what was more inhospitable, the winter chill of the high desert or the company of the heartless criminals within the house. She was the first outside and Arash closed the door behind them.

Hector might've puffed up and postured plenty against the new blood in the gang, but he hadn't lied about the gear in the garage. She'd been too focused on what it meant to be on the compound to take stock of what tools and equipment were laid out for use. It was everything she'd need to turn any nut and bolt on a car.

"I've worked in pro garages with less tech." Arash also checked it all out, hand hovering over the tools like he was sensing their auras.

"You don't need tools. You just use your ear and your nose." She pulled the coveralls over her clothes and rolled the cuffs and sleeves to fit.

He pulled his hair back into a ponytail and donned his own coveralls. "Tell me you smelled that faulty turbo charger, too." The white material accentuated the wide plane of his chest and just how broad his shoulders were.

"Hell, yeah." She found the switches for the overhead lights and turned them all on. "Like someone was frying doughnuts."

He laughed and dragged a pair of ramps in front of the car. As he leaned down to line them up with the tires, she glimpsed the shape of his tight butt. She looked away and tried to reset her mind by calculating the proper order of disassembly. He tapped the hood. "Want to bring it up?"

She climbed into the car and turned the engine over. He motioned her forward, checking low as she eased up the ramps. His closed fist told her to stop and she set the brake and shut the car down.

He kicked a low rolling platform out from under a shelf and nudged it toward the front bumper. While he rummaged for tools, she got out and found a fluorescent work light among other flashlights and headlamps. The greenish glow took her back to the first nights under a car in the maintenance department of her friend's father's auto dealership. Arash took the light from her and lay down on the platform with an array of tools and an empty container for oil on his chest. The work light carved him in half, bright and black. She focused on the shadows to remind herself he wasn't to be trusted.

The glow of the light spread out under the car when he shoved forward on his heels and disappeared beneath the chassis. Metal scraped against metal and the work began. She knew the processes, but not the shop, so it took a moment before she located a siphon and gas can.

While she pumped the fuel out of the car, Arash's voice rang metallic from below. "They had auto shop in private school?"

"My friend's dad had a dealership." The Japanese American girl's relationship with her father had been more stable than Stephanie's family life, leading to many evenings hanging out at the Hirais' house. "We'd wrench on Julie's

Civic in the last bay while the real mechanics were working late."

"Sounds way better than getting crabgrass up your ass while doing neighborhood oil changes in the front yard." He grunted with effort for a second and she heard oil spilling into the receptacle. "I'm going to guess that Julie's out boosting high-end cars, too." His voice boomed, overdramatic. "Your best friend is now your greatest rival."

"She's flying all over the globe as an art dealer." All the gas was siphoned out of the car, so Stephanie capped the can and stowed it with the others.

"You're the one at the reunion with just a photo that says 'Whereabouts Unknown.'" He shifted under the car; more metal clanked.

"A lot of shady kids from shady families at that school." Julie would hate to see Stephanie's performance right now, back on the wrong side of the law. "We only hold reunions on the dark web." Leaving her father's business behind had changed a lot of Stephanie's friendships. She still had her network of information, but it existed with a cool detachment. Julie was one of the only people to stick close with her. College had been a fresh start, though Stephanie had met her fair share of crooks in the economics department.

"I've got a few friends doing a permanent high school reunion at Solano." He dragged himself out from under the car, bringing the tools and full oil container with him.

Because he's a criminal, she reminded herself as she climbed back behind the wheel and tugged the shifter into Neutral. She nodded to Arash when she had her foot on the brake and watched him place his hands on the front of the car and push. The work light shining from the ground carved him into a devil. His muscles flexed, as if he was on top of her, with her legs spread out before him.

She gasped a quick breath and turned her gaze to the interior gauges she would have to dismantle, then released the emergency brake and eased off the pedal. The car rolled backward off the ramps and she locked it down once it settled. Arash rapped his knuckles on the hood, snapping her attention back to him in front of her. She reached under the dash and tugged the hood release.

By the time she came around to Arash, he was stretched out with the hood high. Her shoulder slid against his firm side as she unclipped the support. Swinging it up brought her very close to his face. Close enough for her to stare at his sensuous lips and wonder how damned she'd be if she tasted them.

His eyes burned intense as he stared back at her. And that darkness flickered deep again. Or was it just a trick of the light?

She latched the support into the hood, he released his hold and the two of them parted quickly. It would be easy to blame the Tyvek jumpsuit for the sultry heat that covered her body, but she knew it had more to do with how solid he'd felt against her. And how hungry he'd looked gazing into her eyes.

A sweet aroma enveloped her when he opened the radiator. While the sugary sensation coming from the antifreeze was tempting, she knew that, like Arash, it was deadly. She pulled over an empty jug and he siphoned the thick liquid into it. Instead of watching his body shift with each movement of his arm, she took the work light and hooked it under the hood of the car.

Hoses, pipes and wires banked and curved in a static race through the engine compartment. Down in the center was the stock motor, pierced and bolted through with aftermarket performance additions. She remembered the early days of staring at the puzzle under the hood of Julie's car, neither of them being able to trace cause to effect. But through their diligence, the internet and the mechanics who would wander by to share their expertise, the complications of the engine unwound.

"Here's why you smelled oil." She pointed at the engine and Arash leaned close to her to peer in. "Those fools clocked the turbocharger all wrong, with the return line too high." The circular device could be mounted with several orientations, but only the one with the oil dripping out the bottom was correct.

He shook his head with a disappointed sigh. "Never had a chance." Turning away, he capped the jug of antifreeze and stowed it on a shelf. "At least no one else will have to look at their crap work after this." He returned with his hands held out. Lying on his greasy palms were an array of socket wrenches and screwdrivers.

"Sexy." Damn, she hadn't wanted to say that out loud. Hopefully he thought she was talking about the tools and not his hands. From the burning look he was giving her, he wasn't completely absorbed with automotive motivations. His chest rose and fell, matching the slow pace of her hot breath. She reached forward. He stepped toward her. She could just tilt her head up a little. They were so close.

She licked her lips and took one of the drivers from his hand. He curled his fingers around the rest of the tools. Surprisingly, instead of growing surly, he smiled, intimate and understanding. He leaned into the engine bay and murmured, "If I had my own shop, I'd hire you."

"You couldn't afford me." Hoping the manual work of removing nuts and bolts would cool her down, she started dismantling the first part in front of her.

"I'd only give you the hardest problems." His efforts brought his shoulder close to hers. "The strangest noises, erratic balances, parts that aren't supposed to fit together locked so tight it's like they're meant to be." Each of his words was punctuated by him turning bolts, making him thrust forward and shaking the whole car. And her. "You'd do it just so you could say that you were the only one who figured it out. You'd do it for the pleasure."

She dropped her socket driver and grabbed his wrench. "Stop," she said, more breathless than she wanted. "Stop talking." His face grew serious, but he didn't pull away. "Stop what you're doing." Touching his skin arced a spark straight into her. Heat prickled across her chest, up her neck and into her cheeks. His lips were parted, teeth bared, eyes boring into her. Could she really make him stop? "Stop looking at me that way. And kiss me."

Chapter Seven

He neared her. She tipped her mouth up to meet him. As soon as their lips touched, it would let her know how wrong this was. She'd been trying to convince herself away from him, but she needed this proof. A kiss would blast him out of her system.

She'd been lying to Olesk and his gang. She'd been lying to Arash. And now she was lying to herself.

She tightened her hand on his wrist. He slid his palm over her hip and cupped the small of her back. Their mouths met in an open kiss that stole her breath and had her surging harder into him. He met her force with his own. Hungry and devouring.

Even though layers of clothes separated them, heat blazed where he touched her. Like it could burn away all the lies and leave her naked with her need. She wanted that. Just to give in, as if all the complications didn't exist and it was just her and Arash in one moment. No motives other than pleasure.

He brought their chests together and she dug her fingernails into his wrist. Her body shook as he growled into her mouth. She darted her tongue out to test and tease. He responded immediately with his own tongue, sliding sensuously against hers. Her other hand curled in the fabric on his chest. She pulled him closer. His tongue swept deeper. She could tear his clothes, feel the flesh underneath.

Stephanie broke the kiss and straightened her arm to push him away. His hand slid from her, leaving the heat and making everything surrounding that spot feel far too cold. Fire burned in his eyes and long breaths moved him. She lowered her hand and he maintained the distance. The darkness returned to his face, something like doubt and anger, then he cooled.

She contained the storm within her enough to turn back to the engine and pick up her tools without her hands shaking. Arash resumed his work next to her. Both of them maintained an uncomfortable cushion of space, even in the cramped quarters.

Wrong. She'd been so wrong. The kiss hadn't burned away her need for Arash. It had left her wanting more.

This was bad. Arash hadn't jeopardized his purpose in infiltrating Olesk's gang, but he had guaranteed that when he finally got his revenge, it would be a terrible mess. And it would tear his heart out.

He'd spent too long in the shower, but the heat of the water hadn't chased away the warmth of Stephanie against him. Dressed now in his newly bought clothes, he stood in the middle of his room with the door closed and didn't know how to make the next step. The gang wouldn't question him hooking up with her. She didn't seem to doubt his motivations when they were tangled against each other. But he didn't know what the hell he was doing.

As soon as he'd seen her in those ridiculous coveralls he'd known he wanted to know what she would feel like in his arms and what her mouth would taste like. Her body was only hinted at in the white fabric, but she moved with such confidence. And her fine wrists and hands emerged from the rolled cuffs with such unexpected beauty. Seeing her expertly work on the car with grease on her skin had only turned him on more.

But he couldn't act on it. Though it was tearing him up not to. Flirting around the engine bay was supposed to relieve the pressure, not turn it up. When she told him to kiss her, it was everything he wanted.

And the kiss was hot and hungry and he definitely didn't get enough.

Which was why he was standing behind a closed door and forcing himself into balance before he stepped back into the rest of the house. He double-checked that his folding knife was in his jeans. He'd sharpened it before leaving for the gig in the warehouse. His phone was charged and in his pocket, though he had no one he trusted to reach out to. None of his current friends knew Marcos, and he couldn't drag any of them into this mess. Anyone trying to find him would be calling a phone that was turned off and in a bedside drawer in his apartment. In a day or two his parents would start trying him. His current phone was a burner, and no one except Olesk had the number.

Arash opened the door and moved into the empty hallway. With each step downstairs he hardened himself. The gang wouldn't touch him. And if Stephanie wanted to hold him off after the kiss, all the better. Though he still wanted to burn this house down around Olesk and drag Stephanie free.

But she didn't need rescuing. She was more capable than the rest of these jokers put together. The crew was in one of the living rooms, where Hector and Ellie sat on a couch playing a street racing video game. Olesk was at a nearby table, switching his attention between the game on a bigscreen TV and his phone. Thom perched on the arm of the couch, hands twitching as if he was playing the game.

Stephanie hovered at a distance behind the action with a clouded expression and her arms crossed. She'd also showered and changed and looked fresh enough for a casual night of wine tasting and small plates. Their eyes met and he watched a storm gather behind her gaze. The rest of her remained cool. If the lightning was going to strike, he'd never see it coming. She leaned as if to take a step away from him, but she recovered and stood her ground.

They'd spent the rest of the teardown after the kiss in silence. Hours passed with only necessary words cracking into the still air. But because they both knew their jobs, that meant their voices remained quiet while the tools made all the noise.

"You guys eat dinner?" He could smell food but didn't see any.

"While you two were wrapping up the teardown." Olesk didn't look up from his phone. "Nice work, by the way."

"Thanks." Arash had been on autopilot while boxing and labeling all the parts with Stephanie. Even the seats had been taken out.

"There's plenty of options in the freezer." Olesk waved his hand toward the kitchen.

"Doesn't anyone cook around here?" The pizza had gotten Arash through the day, but it wasn't ideal after wrenching for hours.

Tearing his focus away from his phone, Olesk rolled his eyes. "Feel free to cook. And do the dishes, and keep everything clean. Or just warm something up out of the freezer and save all the trouble."

Arash turned to Stephanie. "You eat?"

"Not yet." She shook her head, mouth tight.

He turned and left the room to the sounds of Ellie gloating a win and Hector's mild outrage. Stephanie walked with him to the kitchen, where he saw the remnants of the crew's dinner boxes piled on a corner of the counter. She opened the freezer and looked over the selection of meals and more pizzas.

She grumbled, "I thought these guys were supposed to be the best of the best. No perks, though."

He pulled out a basic yet substantial meal. "Just because they can drive doesn't mean they have taste. Give me an onion and a steak. I can cook."

"I'd eat that. Pasta with a lot of Parmesan. It's not like a salad's hard to make." She continued to pick through the options.

"Now I'm going to eat a bum-ass Stroganoff and be pissed off all night." He checked the instructions on the package before tearing the cardboard open to get to the cold tray. It went into the microwave and while the timer counted down, he felt his aggravation rising.

After picking out her meal, Stephanie opened the refrigerator. "Beer?"

"Water."

She retrieved two bottles. "Do you drink?"

"Depends on the company." He took one of the waters from her and made a pointed glance back toward the living room. She toasted him with her water and they both drank. So what the hell was this? It didn't feel like they were back to square one, and they certainly weren't racing toward the next kiss. That's what he wanted. Her. That was all kinds of a bad idea. This casual distance was the right way to go, but he knew it wouldn't last. Soon he'd be tearing himself up, wondering if he should tell her about Marcos and what was really at stake here.

The microwave beeped and he dragged his hot tray out to a paper plate. She watched with a distressed look on her face before putting her meal in the machine. As her bowl of some variety spun, Ellie came into the kitchen, with Hector and Thom trailing.

Ellie pulled a beer from the fridge and set it on the island. Thom trundled after her and got two beers, muttering, "Don't you have beer runs in England? It's customary if you're getting up to grab the beers for your friends."

"Oh, we do that for our friends." Dramatically opening her beer with her hands, Ellie took a drink and stared at Thom.

Thom mouthed something under his breath and handed one of the beers to Hector. Ellie pulled two thick envelopes from her hoodie pocket and put them down in front of Arash and Stephanie. "For the teardown," she explained.

Arash took up the envelope and quickly checked over the bills. Another eight grand. "Some of this money should come from Thom and Hector for clocking that turbocharger wrong."

Stephanie eyed Thom coolly as he puffed up and his neck reddened. Ellie outright smiled. Thom set his beer down so hard that it foamed over his fist. "Look here, you little weasel." He showed Arash his teeth. "I don't care what kind of rubber you've laid to get here. You're green in this crew, and you treat me with respect."

Arash straightened and approached Thom. The other man was taller than him, but Arash had more muscle and was very ready to unleash it. He looked Thom dead in the eye. "You should care. I've been a lot of places." Like where Marcos was run off the road, murdered without a chance of living. "And I know a lot of things, Thom." Like as soon as he had his chance, Arash was going to drive all these bastards into the ground. "I earn my cash. You've got to earn my respect."

Thom scowled. His mouth twitched. In a sudden move, he swung the bottle off the island and toward Arash's head. Arash blocked Thom's arm with his own, then slammed his palm into the center of Thom's chest. The taller man skittered backward and slammed to the ground. His beer shattered behind him.

Arash turned on Hector to see if he was going to back his friend up, but Hector just shrugged it off and put a hand out to Thom. Stephanie watched from the edge of the action, though not completely removed. Her body was poised for a fight, but for which side? He wished that Hector would try something. Or lift Thom so Arash could dismantle them both at the same time. Arash balanced on the balls of his feet, ready for so much more.

Once he got up, the red-faced Thom looked like he was willing, though still gasping for breath. But he looked over Arash's shoulder and deflated. Arash checked behind himself to see Olesk casually standing at the edge of the kitchen. A black automatic was tucked into his jeans. "I like trash talk," he said. "But, Thom, don't swing at other members of the crew. Mop it up and make up. You guys are all working on the van project tomorrow. And there might be other things coming."

Arash grabbed his water and plate of food and carried them past Olesk. He settled at a table in the other living room and stared at the cooling tray of Stroganoff. Voices murmured in the kitchen. Broken glass was swept around. Footsteps approached. Stephanie brought her dinner with her and sat at the table with Arash.

He took a long breath to calm enough to eat. Scraping a forkful of food together, he still didn't have the stomach for it. "You had my back?"

"Same as you had my back with him before." Stephanie adjusted the sides of her hair and smiled discreetly.

"No doubt." Why the hell did she have to be part of this bastard gang?

"No doubt." Her smile grew, then disappeared completely.

The voices from the kitchen migrated back to the other living room, where the video game resumed. Marcos had been running with this crew a couple months before they turned on him. There was a possibility he'd been in this house, playing these games. Arash could tell her, right now, about what had happened to his friend. That could change how she feels about Olesk and the STR. She could get out of here before it's too late. Or maybe she already knew. He didn't want to believe Stephanie wouldn't care that these people she now drove with were murderers. But he couldn't count on the glimmers of her ethic pushing her loyalty completely to him.

Arash and Stephanie ate without talking. The frozen meal lost all flavor after the first few bites, but he continued on. When they finished, he took the plates to the overfilled trash in the kitchen before rummaging in the cupboards. Stephanie came in and he slid a package of cookies across the island toward her. "Dessert," he said, wanting her more than the cookies.

She took one and he looked away before he had to watch her take a bite. But he turned his gaze back to her, defying himself and testing his temptation. Her mouth would be sweet with the sugar. She had a little smile. It flickered when she saw him assessing her. She stared back. He pulled a handful of cookies from the package and stepped to her. "The next time you want to kiss me, do it," he said. Yes, the attraction with Stephanie was twisting things way more complicated than he could unknot. But he couldn't ignore it. "And make sure you don't have any plans for the next few hours."

She stared back at him, the heat of desire shimmering behind her cool exterior. Neither moved any closer. She nodded slowly, hands resting on the island. Those fingers would feel so good along his neck and through his hair. He could take her in his arms, lift her up and hold her against him.

He nodded back and left the kitchen. The games continued in the living room as he passed it. No one fired any comments his way. He mounted the stairs and walked to his room alone.

Behind the closed door, he listened to the rush of blood in his ears. The fight with Thom wasn't enough. Olesk flashing his pistol definitely changed the game. Arash would have to take that into account and any other unseen variables when he finally made his move.

The most deadly variable, the one that could wreck him as he hurdled toward revenge, was Stephanie.

Chapter Eight

Stephanie had prepared herself for sleeping under the same roof as criminals. She had her pistol and her knife, and knew how to jam her door using the buckle from her bag's strap. It was part of the mission, a means to ending the Seventh Syndicate's human trafficking. But she hadn't prepared herself for sleeping under the same roof as a man she'd kissed. A man whose heat still resonated where he'd touched her and left her wanting and hungry in the places he hadn't.

Olesk had said they could settle into this area for a while, but she packed her bag anyway, ready to move, before heading downstairs the next morning. It took a few steps for her to coordinate her body. She'd had enough sleep on the mattress on the floor in order to operate, but she didn't feel rested. Any small noise had woken her during the night. And every few minutes, fevered thoughts of Arash sleeping just down the hall would rush through her with cold fire. In a much better world, she would've exchanged the pistol in her bed for another companion.

She was the first one in the kitchen. Empty bottles and the demolished package of cookies from the night before were still on the island. She cleared enough space to prepare her breakfast but stopped before collecting any food. The new sun hadn't broken through the pewter clouds outside the window. It seemed as if a metal lid had been slammed down on top of the world. No escape.

Muted footsteps on the carpeted stairs pushed her into motion. From what she could find, the only available breakfast was cold cereal and drip coffee. She prepped the coffee maker, not bothering to wash the pot, just rinsing out the stale, tinny dregs from the day before. Arash eased into the kitchen, hair down, wearing jeans and a sweatshirt.

The same cold fire that had woken her through the night flashed again. It intensified as he neared. His face was surly, but a softness remained in his eyes as he looked at her. A wry smile curled. "Next time," he said, "I'm joining a gang of interior decorators and chefs."

She pulled two clean cereal bowls from a cupboard and slid them onto the island. "A mattress on the floor is very avant-garde." The refrigerator had several cartons of soy and almond milk. She cracked open a fresh one.

"It's a damn pain." He flexed his back and gave her an all-too-good view of the expanse of his chest and shoulders. "Thanks for getting the coffee going." He put two mugs on the counter.

"Don't thank me and don't blame me." She looked over the selection of cereals and picked the one with the least amount of sugar. The coffee dripped and smelled good enough to tempt her to filling a cup.

"You stayed up?" Arash topped off a bowl with cereal and stood by the coffee maker as it sputtered.

Watching him ascend the stairs last night had been a particular kind of torture. His gravity had pulled at her, as if it would've been easier to rise with him into a private space where they could explore more than just the one kiss. Her body tried to convince her it was the right thing to do, but she knew it would only make things far more complicated. She'd rooted her feet to the ground and locked her muscles. "Had to stay and watch those asses lose to Ellie a while longer."

"I'll be sure not to play against her."

"You're smarter than I thought." Ellie walked into the kitchen wearing a concert T-shirt from a punk band, her hair and makeup already on point.

Arash poured his coffee. "Most ladies think I'm all wrench and no brains." He swaggered to the table by the window with his food. Stephanie remained on the other side of the kitchen. Even when she turned her back to prepare her coffee, the pull to him remained.

Ellie worked around her, collecting a bowl and a mug. "We have a toaster, I'll see about some bread and butter today."

"Sounds civilized." Stephanie toasted Ellie with her mug of coffee.

"Only the finest, love." Ellie dived into her bowl of cereal. Stephanie ate next to her. The clouds outside remained solid gray. Beneath them, Arash hunched over his breakfast. He faced the main path into the kitchen and paused to stare at Hector and Thom as they entered. Neither man acknowledged him and he resumed eating as soon as they went about their breakfast business. Ellie spoke to the room. "I'm walking you through the next stage of the van projects today."

"Engine or body mods?" Stephanie asked.

"Today's body," Ellie answered. "But you're on another detail." She glanced up to where Olesk walked into the kitchen. "Right? Stephanie's behind the wheel?"

Stephanie's gut clenched with the unexpected news, but she kept her exterior smooth. "What's the detail?"

Olesk poured his coffee. Arash didn't move and watched intently. After stirring his coffee and tossing the plastic spoon in the trash, Olesk turned to Stephanie. "We have a client who needs a driver. In town only. I'm taking you in to pick up the car after breakfast."

She'd heard the STR did this kind of work and was prepared. But the idea of leaving Arash alone on the compound was unexpectedly distressing. He hadn't backed down from any conflicts with Thom, and things could escalate quickly. It also meant she'd be heading into the unknown without the only ally she had in this mess. "Are we pulling a job? Do I need to plan escape routes and contingencies?"

"Nah." Olesk waved off the idea. "There was no mention of it and the contract price doesn't cover it. If he escalates to that, feel free to negotiate a new rate."

"Sounds good." At least her job of gaining their trust was going well.

"Sweet. Five minutes." Olesk took his coffee out of the kitchen, and Ellie followed him.

Hector asked Thom as they collected their breakfasts, "How much do you love body work?"

"More than I love your mother," Thom grumbled.

"Nobody gets to say anything about *mi madre*." Hector cocked his head with a casual smile.

Thom screwed up his face, disbelieving. "It was a joke."

"I hate clowns." Hector carried his food toward the table where Arash sat. Arash got up before he arrived and passed both men on the way to the sink.

When he was next to her, Arash spoke under his breath, "Careful out there."

She nodded. The pistol was already holstered and hidden by her jacket. "Careful in here," she whispered.

He turned and locked eyes with her. This was trouble. The same electricity between them that had preceded the kiss. Like lightning before the tornado. It would take less than a step to close the distance. Just one touch to reassure he was looking out for her, and for her to tell him she didn't want him hurt. Neither moved. Arash winked at her and smiled with wicked confidence.

Their gazes broke when he spun and walked toward the mudroom. "We doing this or what?" He rallied the house. Hector kept eating and Thom flipped him off. Arash didn't break stride and disappeared behind the mudroom door.

A moment later, she saw him walking outside the house. He clutched his collar tight as what looked like a cold wind pushed his hair back. Hector spotted him, too, and waved with ironic exaggerated joy. Thom just sneered. Arash gave them the finger and proceeded toward the two white passenger vans parked near the barn where they had torn down the car yesterday.

Ellie breezed through the kitchen. "The sooner we finish this, the sooner we can get to the engines." That energized Hector and Thom to leave their dirty bowls on the table and follow her into the mudroom.

Olesk stood on the other side of the kitchen, keys jingling in his hand. "Ready?"

She had to be ready. No matter what was coming, it was taking her one step closer to her goal. "Let's go."

The wind outside was as cold as it had looked. The clouds continued to clamp down on the sunlight, diffusing the shadows and softening the landscape. Olesk wove through the selection of cars at the front of the house until he reached a bland four-door sedan. He climbed behind the wheel and started the engine before she was fully into the passenger seat. "Twenty minutes," he said, checking his watch.

She heard the rolling door of the cargo truck open behind the house, then closed her own door as Olesk stood on the gas. Dirt and gravel sprayed out behind the car as it jumped forward. She shouldn't have been surprised his ordinary car hid a supercharged engine. They sped down the driveway toward the road. She might never make it back to this compound. Or if she did, she might never see Arash again. That was the kind of people she was dealing with. Death came faster than the firing of a spark plug.

Olesk turned onto the road with deliberate movements. He operated with almost mechanical precision, a contrast to his usual casual attitude. Within the car, he was in constant motion: checking the mirrors, steering, double-checking the shifter knob, even though it was an automatic. His face was motionless, as if he didn't need it for human interaction now that he was driving.

"Music?" She reached for the radio as a test.

"No." He held up his finger in a warning, then adjusted the rearview mirror. An important tell. He loved control, and that could be his weakness. If she ever had to take him on, the best thing she could do to frustrate him was something unexpected and illogical.

"Can I get the setup on who I'm driving, or is this another surprise?" The worst surprise would be her father, but she knew he had his own drivers and wouldn't mess with an outside gang like the STR.

Olesk's head twitched to the side, as if he was annoyed by anything other than driving. He checked his watch and answered, "Grant Hemmings." She knew the name. It iced her spine. "He's part of a very important client group of ours, the Seventh Syndicate."

"I've heard of them." And she was more than ready to cut right into their heart. "But I've never worked for them."

"Of course you haven't," Olesk scoffed. "I would've heard of you before this. You're in a whole other league now."

"I hope you know I appreciate this." She cringed internally for having to play nice, then prepared herself for much more of the same.

"I know you do." He tried a smile, but it looked more like a grimace. "The people who don't appreciate what we do don't last as long as you already have." Menace shook in his voice and he blinked rapidly. She'd heard plenty of rumors about how good the STR were at theft, modding cars and getaway driving, but never anything about them rubbing someone out. The constant cold trickle of fear for Arash at the compound turned to a steady rain.

Olesk clammed up and drove, leaving no more openings for conversation. She wasn't going to press him anyway. Any information would need to be taken out surgically, between the nerves so no one knew. Outright curiosity would get her killed.

The rural road led them back into the suburbs, then the city. Nearly twenty minutes to the button after Olesk had called it, he pulled them into a three-story parking structure next to a small office building. On the second floor, he brought the car to a stop next to another four-door sedan, this one with dark tinted windows. As soon as they came to a stop, a white man in his fifties got out of the sedan. He was dressed casually in jeans and a puffy winter jacket, though from the slick cut of his black hair and his shaved face, he looked like he lived most of his life in a tailored suit.

Olesk bounced out of the driver's seat with his hand extended. "Grant."

"Ronald." Grant Hemmings shook hands with business-like efficiency. The man's eyes slid over to her. "This is my driver?"

Olesk nodded graciously. "Stephanie. Not Steph. Stephanie."

Grant didn't approach her and she didn't hold out her hand. The Syndicate man looked her up and down slowly, like he was used to taking whatever he wanted and peeling it apart at his leisure. She gazed back at him defiantly. Playing nice didn't include demeaning herself. Grant kept his look on her as he spoke to Olesk. "You didn't tell me she was armed."

"She isn't." Olesk balked.

Grant turned to him with a placating smile. "Sure she isn't." The Syndicate man put his hand on Olesk's shoulder and started to walk him to a high corner of the parking level. Grant paused and told Stephanie, "Why don't you stand watch. Pretend like you're on the phone or something."

She tipped her head in understanding and pulled out her phone before walking in the opposite direction. Grant resumed his move with Olesk and they were soon out of earshot. She took up a position, with a pillar acting as a windbreak from the chill. Fiddling with her phone, she surreptitiously took several photos of Grant and Olesk's conversation.

Their posture was casual enough; there was no trouble. But there was business. Grant motioned to his watch and counted out numbers in his palm. This was the big gig. This was the human trafficking that Stephanie had to stop. Olesk was getting some of his marching orders. She could finally start planning how her operation might play out.

But she couldn't send the photos or any of what she knew to the rest of Frontier Justice. There was still too much scrutiny and there could be no record of outgoing numbers on her phone. For now, she was still completely isolated, and that kept a constant tight knot at the base of her skull.

Grant gave Olesk a thump on the arm and the two of them walked back toward the cars. Stephanie joined them and saw Olesk deep in thoughts and calculations. He surfaced enough to tell her, "I'll pick you up at the end of your day. No need to get in touch." With that, he was in his car and driving away without any more goodbyes or acknowledgments.

"That guy plans a perfect job." Grant chuckled and

walked to the rear passenger side of his sedan. "And runs it like an atomic clock." He got in and she slid behind the wheel, adjusting the seat for the perfect position. Grant kicked back in the rear seat. "Never seen a better driver, but he doesn't know it all, you know what I mean?"

"I think I do." She'd gone the entire time with no one in the STR knowing she was armed, but Grant had been immediately aware.

He leaned forward, arm on the back of her chair and face so close she could smell his aftershave. "What about you? Do you just drive?" His voice was a little too sticky, and she would've liked to throw her elbow back into his smarmy grin.

"That's what I'm getting paid for." She held him off with a firm tone. "Just driving."

"Good to know." He leaned back, voice neutral, but the grin was still on his face. "Today, I've got work and I've got play." He took out his phone and read an address. She plugged it into the navigation app on her phone. "We start with work."

Stephanie turned the engine over and brought all her mental facilities in line. Every detail she could pick up during this day would help her mission. And any slipups could kill her. For the next unknown span of time, she had to ride with one of the monsters she was dedicated to taking down.

Chapter Nine

The clouds pressed closer over Arash. Suffocating. The sun never broke through and there was no relief from the dread surrounding him. He worked as efficiently as he could while watching his back and hating that he had no idea where Stephanie was or what she was doing.

The first job of the day was drilling out the floor panels of the two vans so they could attach four rows of seats in each. He now knew that whatever the coming gig was, they would be moving people. And these people either weren't supposed to be seen, or were to be kept from knowing their location. Or both. There were no windows in the vans except at the front. From the exterior, they were all white sheet metal and looked like something for a utility worker or tradesman.

A welder hissed and spattered outside as Hector and Thom prepped the bench seats. They muttered behind their masks and dragged their materials around, but they did solid work at the end. Arash punched the last hole in the floor panel and stepped out of the van with his tools. "Next?"

"Can you weld?" Ellie had been hovering close to keep things moving and checked over a list on her phone.

"I get by." He wasn't a master, but he knew enough for repairs.

"No." Hector stopped welding and lifted his helmet. "No, he can't. Only I weld."

Thom yanked up his mask with a pout. "Hey, I'm gonna—"

"You're not." Hector turned on him. "None of you jokers are qualified. You'll lay down a bad bead, then as soon as we take a hard turn, everything goes to hell." He pointed with his gloved hand to Ellie. "No one welds but me."

"Fine. They prep, you weld." She waved Arash toward a tall stack of black-painted sheet steel with a sketched diagram taped to the top. "Lay the pieces out in this order on those sawhorses."

"But don't clamp anything down." Hector lowered his mask and resumed welding. Two of the bench seats had already been completed. Arash saw that Hector had attached steel rings to the metal frames on each side. Perfect for shackles. Arash's stomach dropped and swirled with sickening acid. Whoever was being transported, they weren't VIPs.

He tried to hide his expression with the effort of organizing the sheet steel. Most of it was solid, but there was a perimeter of open grate around it. The dimensions were perfect for creating a partition between whoever was in the seats and the front of the van. He swallowed the rising bile and asked Ellie, "So you know what this gig is?" Any details would help him plan how to take down Olesk and the STR. Multiple drivers in multiple vans would complicate things, but that also meant they might be thinned out and could be taken on one at a time.

"I do." She remained cagey. "Right now the gig is laying this work out."

He double-checked the diagram and saw that the pieces were all in place. "Angle grinder?"

Hector stopped welding but kept his mask down. "What are you going to mess up?"

Arash balled a fist, then released it. How long was he going to have to dance with these tarantulas before he could step on them? At least he didn't have to play nice. He moved toward Hector. "I was going to grind the paint off where the welds are supposed to go, but if you want to do garbage work, feel free."

Hector tipped his mask up and pointed at Arash with the welding gun. "I never do garbage work."

"Then you don't weld through paint." Arash didn't back down. "Do you?" The muscles in Hector's neck jumped and his jaw flexed. Thom stood at the ready next to him, his mouth moving but not forming words. Arash would go for Hector first. Thom looked like he hit hard, but he didn't have too much meat on his bones and probably couldn't take too many punches. The pressure built and Arash was so ready to break bones.

"If we don't get this work done on time," Ellie sliced through the tension with her dagger-sharp voice, "the gig fails. No one gets paid. The lucky ones might get dead. And the unlucky ones spend the rest of their lives looking over their shoulder."

Those were higher stakes than anything he'd heard of from the STR. Marcos's death was definitely unusual for the driving crew. The client for this gig created a brutal ethic. Arash shook out his arms to loosen them and turned to Ellie. "Angle grinder?"

"You'll find all that in the shop." She tipped her head to the second barn.

He walked that way, longing for the moment when his boots crunching on dirt was the only sound in the world. Like he was walking away from the smoking wreck of Olesk and his gang. In Arash's imagination, another set of footsteps joined him. Stephanie, clear from danger and finally safe, strode with him.

The electric gnashing of the welder behind him erased

the victorious image from Arash's mind. There was no safety. He was stuck pretending to be part of the gang while building rolling prisons for people he didn't know. Stephanie was out in the unknown, where he couldn't help her.

STEPHANIE KNEW CRIME. She'd grown up in it, had seen the unmarked envelopes passed to her father, the unexpected meetings he had to take in the back of the restaurant during dinner, the stress that went beyond normal life and into the territory of betrayal, and the consequences of the law. Sitting in the front seat of Grant's sedan, waiting for him to finish the second of this morning's business meetings, she wondered how many people walking down this sidewalk or driving on this street recognized what was going on right next to them. She saw it. Even if she hadn't been driving for one of the worst criminal organizations in the nation that day, she would've known something was wrong by the way they circled blocks and doubled back, throwing any potential tails before pulling up to nondescript brick buildings with empty storefronts and a dental office.

But no one looked twice at her, and she knew there'd been no tails on the vehicle. She leaned back casually and scrolled over her phone. Anyone, including Grant Hemmings, would think she was looking at social media pictures of food. But it was code, in public sight. Frontier Justice had set up several fake accounts where they could place messages. Each member had been assigned a stand-in. Because Mariana Balducci's apple orchard was where the original Frontier Justice and this new iteration had started, her code image was apples. Ty had picked potatoes, and Vincent went with grapes. Of course Javier was a banana. But none of these showed up on the feed of the app. There was only one image from a fake account, of peaches, the code she'd picked to identify herself. The comment below read, "Winter is getting me down. I don't know where to find any peaches."

They didn't know where she was. And she couldn't tell them. If someone got into her phone and found she'd responded to this post with her location, they'd know she was double-dealing.

Grant came out of the dentist's office and checked over the sidewalk before stepping toward the car. He seemed preoccupied, and she imagined this meeting kept building the details for the coming gig. She took her time shutting down the app and stowing her phone so she didn't look hurried and suspicious. "Where to next?" she asked as he climbed into the back seat.

He wasn't done processing his thoughts and took out his phone and typed without answering. After a few moments, he tossed his phone next to him and looked at her through the rearview mirror. "I'm starving."

She started the car and pulled out into the flow of traffic. "Any place in mind?" Her own blood sugar was plunging, but she couldn't let it affect her performance on the job. The idea of driving aimlessly through a city she didn't know in search of a place that would satisfy the sociopath in the back seat ground her patience to a razor's edge.

Grant rubbed his hands together. "Sonny's Steak and Seafood." He rattled off the address. "Always hit them up when I'm in town."

She plugged the address into her phone at the next stoplight, then wove her way through town in an unpredictable route. Grant was back on his phone, face blank. There was so much information she had to get to Frontier Justice, including this restaurant now, but she had to wait with her teeth grinding.

After a few minutes and zero tails or suspicious eyes on them, she arrived at the low building with a discreet sign carved into a piece of weathered wood. The place looked like it had been built in the sixties. A pitched roof lay over a lava-stone facade with no windows. A single large lantern with amber glass swung gently in the breeze near the thick wood doors. Grant leaned forward with a fifty-dollar bill between his fingers. "You can take the car to get your own lunch, but get it to go and stick close."

"You've got it." She took the money and gave him a little salute with it. He nodded with a smirk, got out of the car and slid quickly into the restaurant. Eluding Arash at the mall long enough to get the burner phone and send a couple messages had barely worked. Her cover story had held up for him, but she knew Grant wouldn't tolerate any variance from his sphere of safety. Until she could figure out some other way to contact Frontier Justice, she had to act the part of the perfect criminal syndicate driver.

She pulled onto the street and drove in expanding rings around the steakhouse until she found a strip mall with something other than a chain restaurant. The spiced aromas from an empanada place led her from the parking lot and through the front doors. There were a couple occupied tall round tables, but it was clear from the wide counter and mass of people waiting that most of the business was takeout.

A dark-haired Latina woman behind the register smiled warmly when Stephanie approached. "Welcome in." Stephanie knew that the woman probably said it to most people, but it felt so genuine that tears nearly welled in Stephanie's eyes. All of her recent interactions had been so hazardous that she'd forgotten what it was like to simply make eye contact with another human and exchange smiles. The times she'd found that with Arash had been tinged with too much danger to feed her soul the way this casual interaction had. The woman continued, "What can I get for you?"

Stephanie stared at the handwritten menu above the counter and nearly told her to get in touch with Frontier

Justice and tell them that Grant Hemmings of the Seventh Syndicate is in Reno while the STR are northeast of the city on a compound getting ready for the big gig. "One beef, one chicken and one chard to go."

"Excellent." The woman rang her up and pointed to the refrigerator case on the side wall. "Drink?" Stephanie made her selection and picked up two cellophane bags of dulce de leche cookies. The woman smiled knowingly and came up with a final total. The fifty-dollar bill more than covered it and Stephanie soon had a handful of change. A few of the bills went into the tip jar, the rest into her jacket pocket.

The lunch crowd continued behind Stephanie and she moved into the mix of people waiting for their orders. The numbers were called out and the group ebbed and flowed for a few minutes until she was up. The woman behind the counter had dealt with at least half a dozen people by the time Stephanie left. Their brief and basic interaction had probably been forgotten. No one in the place would remember Stephanie if she disappeared at the end of the day. Hell, she might not even make it through the next two hours.

Cold wind cut her outside. The heat from the to-go container in her hands was the only remnant of the positive feelings she'd gathered in the restaurant. She got into the sedan, started it and didn't move. It had nearly a full tank of gas and plenty of power. Standing on the throttle would rocket her out of Reno. But she had to stay. Her mission wasn't over. And no matter how many times she told herself he was just another crook in the gang, she couldn't leave without knowing if the heart she saw in Arash was real.

HE WAS BUILDING a cage. The bench seats with their additional shackle points had been bolted down to the floor panels, and Arash now positioned one of the steel walls just behind the cab of the van. There was no door in the wall. Whoever went into this van was trapped.

The metal was still warm from Hector's welds. He and Arash had stayed out of each other's way for most of the build, but there had been plenty of hard looks from Thom.

The others didn't seem to be bothered by the implications of what they constructed. It was just a job to them, like adding a tow hitch on a pickup truck or lowered struts on a street cruiser. Arash hadn't forgotten what Olesk had said about someone growing a conscience. Marcos had learned what this gig was, and he couldn't stomach it. But no one walked away from anything this big. Arash had to keep his ethic to himself in order to stay on with the STR, and it was eating away at his sanity.

The impact driver rattled in his hand. Each bolt down made the cage more complete. The wall was strong enough to hold back a person throwing themselves at it. Arash eyed the open side doors of the van and felt his breath grow faster. As if he was sealed in and running out of air. But he kept shooting the bolts through the flanges Hector had welded in. The panic ratcheted higher with each knock of the driver. He would have to warn Stephanie about this space when she got back.

If she got back.

He finished securing the front wall and hopped out of the van, chest heaving. Stephanie might already know about the cage in the van. If he showed her his feelings about it, she could rat him out to Olesk. Though he still didn't know how her hints at an ethic lined up with any of this. Could she really be blinded by the cash? But how clean was he? Throughout the day he'd done perfect work securing the benches and the walls. No one was getting out of those vans because of what he had already done. Was this the price of his revenge?

Chapter Ten

The brief peace Stephanie had created while eating the empanadas and hoarding the feeling from the restaurant was shattered when Grant Hemmings skipped out of the steakhouse. She'd parked at the curb where she'd dropped him off and he slipped easily into the back seat. His eyes swam slightly and he brought the sharp aroma of gin with him. A loose grin looked more like a sneer. "Best steak in town," he slurred. "You eat?"

"I did, thank you." She pulled the bills from her jacket pocket. "Your change."

Grant leaned forward, his eyes sliding from the money to her hand, then down her arm and to her chest. He licked his lips. "Keep it. You weren't going to give all of it to me anyway." He was right; she'd skimmed ten off the top. His gaze lingered too long on her body, then moved to her face. "Do you play?" She knew his leer, had seen it on countless men. Like he was untouchable and could touch anything or anyone he wanted. Like every woman in the world wanted him.

"I drive." She gave him nothing. If she'd released her revulsion and anger, it would've been in a swift blow to his throat.

He blew out a disappointed breath and she smelled the pickled olives of his gimlets. "I'll bet you're a great driver."

Sulking, he leaned back into the seat and thankfully away from her.

"I am. Don't worry." She threw the car in gear to indicate it was time to move on. "You're getting what you paid for."

"Then drive." He waved his hand with disappointment. She pulled onto the street and checked in the rearview mirror to see Grant staring out the side window, eyelids low and head rocking from side to side. Whether or not he was on time to his next appointment wasn't her problem, so she took the car deeper into the city, conscious of doubling back and turning unexpectedly at times to shake any potential tails.

After seven blocks of silence, Grant took out his phone and rattled off an address. She plugged it into her nav and headed that way. "We're late," he growled, surly. "Hurry up." So his drunk lunch had become her responsibility to fix.

"I'm to wait outside?" She urged the car faster and neared the destination.

"Yeah," he spat. "You wait outside and then you drive me to the next one. That's what you're paid to do, right?"

"You paid for the best and you got the best." The more sullen he became, the more cool water she drew from her well. She pulled up to the destination and remained facing forward. Grant organized himself, took a deep breath that didn't brighten his face and stepped out, still showing some of the effects of the booze. He didn't bother saying anything before slamming the car door and walking into the two-story business building with a smoked glass facade.

Another business meeting, another address she needed to relay to Frontier Justice. The Seventh Syndicate had kept their information regarding the human trafficking airtight. No leaks had hit her network or Vincent's FBI contacts. Infiltrating the STR had already given Stephanie more intel than anyone had been able to collect. But it didn't do any good if she couldn't get the word out. There wasn't even a sketchy-looking pay phone within view. Someone in this town must know where those nearly extinct phones were, but she was at a loss unless on her home turf in San Francisco.

She turned the ring around her finger and breathed to slow time. Right now her job was driving Grant and collecting as many details as she could. He returned to the car a few minutes later. Whatever had happened in the meeting had erased his smug grin and replaced it with a sober, dark look on his face.

"I can't be late to this next meeting. We're about an hour away." He read off an address in Incline Village, a very expensive neighborhood she knew on the north shore of Lake Tahoe. Friends of her family had multimillion-dollar second homes there that stood empty for most of the year.

"I'll get you there." She hit the gas and aimed for the highway south. Grant's new quiet persisted. He just watched the passing scenery, and she imagined that he'd been dressed down for showing up to the meeting with a buzz. She made a definite note that whoever held an office in the glass building outranked Grant.

They quickly blew out of the city and the mountains churned around them. As she drove she organized her information by importance, so if she had a limited opportunity to get the word out, she'd relay the hottest intel first. Frontier Justice would have a lot to work with. But she remained in the dark. Especially with Arash. She'd given his name to Vincent and Ty when she'd reached out with the burner phone, but she hadn't been able to receive anything they might've found. She didn't need a dossier on Olesk and the others to know which side they were on. A profile on Arash was necessary. Yes, because she'd kissed him. But also because she still couldn't place how his morality and sensibility fit in with the gang. Which was why she was able to kiss him in the first place. And damn it, it was still moving her, like a wave that had receded to gather strength before slamming back.

The closer they drove to the lake, the more nervous Grant became. He shifted from one side of the car to the other to look out the window, and checked his phone every minute. She was sure there were no pursuers, on the road or in the air, but he still bent his neck to watch the sky for a mile. She tried to keep his manic energy from creeping into her. If he was headed for real trouble, it could be bad for her, as well. The Syndicate wouldn't think twice about erasing a driver if they were willing to rub out one of their own. Her pistol remained close at her back.

She reassured herself with the idea that if they really wanted to make Grant disappear, they wouldn't go through the trouble of having a day's worth of meetings first. Unless they needed to debrief him for all his info before they didn't need him anymore.

Grant's tight voice announced, "Coming up on the left." She pulled onto a country road that cut along a high hill. Below, the lake shined like polished steel under the gray clouds. Winter had tightened the land with cold, but the snow hadn't arrived yet.

The properties spread out with acres between them. She turned off the road and onto a long paved driveway that snaked higher. They cleared a stand of pine trees and were presented by a three-story house built into the side of the hill. Clean glass, blond wood and polished concrete came together in modern angles that overlooked the lake and mountains beyond.

She pulled into a circular parking area at the second level of the house and came to a stop among three SUVs and one other sedan, each one with a driver standing nearby. "We're a little early," she told Grant.

He smiled, but it didn't last. "Early is on time for these

guys. Good job." She saw the nerves still rattling him and fought to maintain her own calm. Without another word, he stepped out of the car and walked to the house. A white man in a suit inside the house opened the door for him and then he disappeared.

Brisk mountain air filled the car through the open side door. The chill needled her exposed skin, but the freshness was welcome. She got out of the car and moved around the side to close the passenger door. Each step released the scent of pine from dry needles under her boots.

It would've been a beautiful spot, except for the hard stares from the four other drivers. Three white men and one black man, all under the age of thirty-five and filling out their casual-yet-pressed clothes with able muscles. She could see from the way their arms hung that they were all concealing weapons. Pistols, at least. One of the men could've fit a submachine gun under his coat.

She gazed back at them. Not enough to challenge, but to state that she was not intimidated and belonged there as much as they did. The silent communication lasted only that long. The men turned back to their individual meditations, leaning against the sides or tailgates of their cars. She suppressed a secret laugh. These men wouldn't be acting so casual if they really knew who she was. Hell, some of them might've been shooting at her not that long ago in an expensive San Jose neighborhood. Her face had remained hidden during that operation. After this, everyone would know. But that was just fine. She looked forward to the time when Seventh Syndicate men panicked every time they saw her coming.

Just like her first ancestor to come to California, she stood with a stick of dynamite in one hand and a match in the other. It was just a matter of time and opportunity until she lit the fuse.

Before she could blast it all apart, she spent her time

imprinting the cars and men on her memory. The house's location was recorded and put to the top of the list. Pictures would've been gold, but she knew taking her phone out now, even to look like she was casually bored, would spark suspicion. There were two trash cans at the edge of the driveway she was dying to dig through for more details, but she would have to leave that work to the bears and raccoons in the area.

She made her face a neutral mask and leaned on the front fender of the sedan to stare down at the lake. But she kept all the men in her peripheral vision. The house had a broad porch on the top floor. If anyone came out there to get a shot at her, she'd see them coming and could duck into the trees at the edge of the driveway. That cover would give her the best chance of surviving a pursuit. Sunset wasn't for a couple hours, so she couldn't rely on darkness hiding her. She'd have to fight her way off this hill.

More time passed. Boredom slouched the postures of the other drivers. A couple of them smoked. One did push-ups on the side of his car. She picked up a dry twig and rolled it between her fingers. Flaking bark made a landscape across the surface, tiny topography that she traced and discovered. If she'd been alone she would've used her knife to whittle one end into a point. But she didn't really want to be alone up on this hill. This was a view to be shared. What would Arash think about it? She knew he'd driven the mountain pass, but she wasn't sure if he'd ever ventured into the wilderness.

The front door of the house opened and all the drivers, including her, snapped alert. She dropped the stick and moved to stand by the rear passenger door. The first man out of the house was tall and white, with a fringe of hair around his mostly bald head. She didn't recognize him, but memorized the pattern of gold rings on his fingers. He stooped into one of the SUVs and that driver whisked him off the property.

Grant was the second one out of the house. She was desperate to see the others who emerged, but she had to do her job and opened the car door for him. He was quickly into his seat and staring forward, ready to go. She got behind the wheel, feeling how his dour energy had transformed to his old upbeat self. Once they were away from the house and on the drive to the side road, he leaned forward with that smarmy grin. "There's a really nice hotel here with incredible views of the lake. What do you say we go?"

"I can get you there and wait in the car." She remained all business.

"Harsh." He sat back and pulled out his phone. "It's not just about me, you know. I'd give you a great time. A great time. Understand? Like you'd want to come back."

"I'd be happy to come back, if you ever need a driver again." He was on the edge of aggression and she had to tread carefully. "It's what I'm best at."

After grumbling, "We could change that," he stared out the window. The sun sank below the clouds to skip along the peaks of the mountains. Gold light flickered against a deep black void. Stephanie navigated onto the highway north and Grant spoke up with another address. She put it in her nav and her memory.

The clouds lit on fire, then darkness took over the land as she and Grant slipped back toward Reno. Traffic thickened. At night, the cars were reduced to their headlights, forcing her to be extra diligent about tracking any potential tails. She maneuvered through the city while Grant remained quiet behind her. Spending the day on edge had burned through her energy and she rallied to stay alert. Dinner would help, but she had no idea what was next, or how long she'd have to pretend that she didn't want to wring Grant's neck until he gave up all the information on human trafficking.

They reached their destination and she moved the address lower on her mental list. It was a strip club. A wide, cracked parking lot spread in front of the low building. Flashing yellow lights surrounded the sign. The Gold Rush. The same lights lined the underside of the awning, drawing men to the front door. There was a decent flow of patrons, but not enough to facilitate a bouncer outside the front door. She imagined that the cover was taken and IDs checked just inside.

"Want to see the show?" Grant flashed a roll of cash from his jacket pocket. "I'll cover your door charge, but I won't pay for any of your lap dances."

"I'd hate to cheat on my favorite ladies up in North Beach." A night watching her friends dance would definitely beat another second spent with Grant. "Another time. Thanks."

He clicked his tongue and shook his head with disappointment. "At least you're a good driver. Stick close." With a heavy sigh, he swept from the car. A few steps across the parking lot and his posture changed, bouncing higher with excitement.

The steel bands across her chest lifted when Grant disappeared into the club. She breathed and turned the ring on her finger. Of course there was a pay phone on the side of the strip club, but because she didn't know how long Grant would be, she couldn't risk getting caught on it.

She busied herself with her cell phone. No messages from Olesk. She tightened again, not knowing what was happening on the compound to the north. They were supposed to be working on the vans, but from the way Arash was sparking off of Thom, things could be very bloody by now.

The layout of Reno and the territory north was familiar

enough to her now that she could speed back to the compound without looking at directions. But was she needed there? Arash wanted to join the gang, even if she didn't want to believe he fit in there. He didn't back down from Thom, but Arash seemed too smart to push things too far and jeopardize his position in the STR.

Scrolling through the false social media accounts she saw more mentions of peaches. She had so much to tell Frontier Justice. There was another access point in a fan fiction chat board where they used coded language, but even that was closed to her responding to her teammates until she could get a phone with no trace.

The wad of cash Grant had shown her could keep him in the club for hours. With the sun down, she lost track of the progress of time. The artificial flashing yellow lights continued. It could be three in the morning or nine o'clock at night. The parking lot grew busier. Her watch told her it was just after six in the evening.

But it was late enough for the three men nearing her car to be weaving on drunken legs. They were white, with gym bodies and expensive sneakers. Extra loud laughs barked into the night, interspersed with joking insults. They jostled each other and staggered when knocked into. One of them, wearing a throwback football jersey for a long-retired player from a team in another state, was quick to punch the others in the shoulder whenever they touched him. His friend in the leather jacket brushed off the blows, but the man in the quilted puffer set his jaw and made a fist at the football jersey guy.

Football jersey guy lunged like he was coming after the man in the puffer, making him flinch and stumble backward into Stephanie's car. The other two men laughed mockingly. She took a long breath to stay steady. When Puffer Jacket saw the car was occupied, he put his hands out. "Sorry,

sorry," he slurred. His eyes widened when he really looked at her. "Let me make sure I didn't dent anything."

"It's no problem." She waved him off. "You guys have a great evening."

"We can't just leave you out here alone. We'll walk you to the door." Football Jersey stepped closer to her closed window.

"I'm staying right where I am, thanks." After this day with Grant, her patience was as thin as a garrote.

Leather Jacket spoke up. "You're not dancing tonight?"

"Not tonight, sorry." All three men now crowded next to her door. "But there are plenty of lovely ladies just inside."

Puffer Jacket propped his elbow on the roof of the car. "None of them are going to be as pretty as you." He smiled like he was the nicest guy in the world.

"What about a private dance?" Football Jersey dug a stack of bills from his front pocket. "I'll pay for it."

"My boss wouldn't like that." She tried to keep her voice firm and even. "I'm already on the clock." Flashing her pistol was an option, but these fools would probably be so pissed by her rejection that they'd tell whoever was running security inside.

Leather Jacket waved off her words. "We won't tell him. It'll be your side hustle and you'll make some cash." He, too, had a handful of bills. Mostly ones. She also spotted a folding knife clipped to the interior of his jeans' pocket. "Dance out here. I can beatbox."

"Yeah!" Puffer Jacket lit up like he loved the idea. "He'll beatbox."

The three men would not let up. Football Jersey knocked on the window slowly. "Fine. Don't do it for the cash. Do it to get back at Daddy. You all have daddy issues, right?"

She threw the door open, slamming its edge into the side of Puffer Jacket's face. He reeled to the side and knocked into Football Jersey. The two men stumbled far enough that she could open the door completely and step out to face the man in the leather jacket.

Shock quickly turned to rage on his face. "What the hell is your problem, you psycho bi—" She stopped his last word with a slap across his face. He winced and blinked, surprised. Then he made a fist and swung at her.

She sidestepped and kicked him quickly in the shin, then the side of the knee. He buckled to the ground with a yelp. By then, Football Jersey had righted himself and came at her, arms outstretched like he was going to wrap her up.

Ducking under his attempt, she drove the heel of her hand up beneath his chin. Her body shook with the impact against the larger man. His head snapped back and his momentum carried him into the side of Grant's sedan. Football Jersey coughed and braced himself on the fender. She slid close and jabbed her fist quickly into his armpit. He screamed out and his arm locked to his side.

While spinning to see if either of the other men were coming, she felt the cell phone in the back pocket of Football Jersey's jeans. She wanted it, but she had to wait as Puffer Jacket leaped at her, shoulder first. He still held a hand over his forehead where the car door had opened a small cut. She released all the tension that had been building throughout the day in a whipping kick that caught him in the stomach. Gasping, he lurched forward and all his momentum carried him into Football Jersey's back.

She was thrown off balance by the kick and skidded sideways next to the two men. She gathered herself enough to grab Football Jersey's phone and slip it into her jacket pocket before separating from them and letting the two tangle to the ground.

Leather Jacket watched his friends go down with red, watery eyes. That hateful gaze snapped to her and he came on strong, despite the limp. She tried to reposition herself to avoid the attack, but Football Jersey reached out and grabbed her ankle.

A fist from Leather Jacket flew close and she could only lean to get away. The blow grazed her shoulder, adding to the anger that boiled through her from being gripped by Football Jersey. She twisted, throwing her elbow into Leather Jacket's jaw. He hit the ground hard, barely conscious.

She gritted her teeth, raised her free foot up and smashed the heel of her boot down on Football Jersey's wrist. Bones broke and he screamed. Puffer Jacket kicked away from Football Jersey and rose to his feet on wobbly legs. He sneered and pulled the folding knife from his pocket. The blade flicked out and glinted in the flashing yellow lights of the strip club.

The man was reckless, weaving the knife back and forth in front of him as if it intimidated her. She channeled her emotions to focus on the danger before her. He was a few paces away; she could time his attack if she had to. She smiled with malice and drew her own knife. A push of a lever brought the spring-loaded blade out the front with a secure snap.

The fight drained out of the man and he lowered his knife while staring at hers.

"I thought you wanted to dance." She took a step toward him.

He bolted without a second glance at his friends on the ground. She retracted the blade on her knife and held it in a shaking hand. Adrenaline bounced with electric-white flares through her. A figure walked toward her across the parking lot, silhouetted against the flashing lights. She prepared herself for another conflict.

But it was Grant, grinning like he'd just won a prize. "You told me you just drove."

"For money," she explained. She moved to the rear of the

car and opened the door for him. He got in and she stepped around Football Jersey and Leather Jacket to climb back behind the wheel. "I did this for free."

Grant chuckled and craned his neck to look down at the fallen men. "I wish I'd seen the whole thing." Relief threaded through her. He probably hadn't seen her pocket Football Jersey's phone. "Get us out of here. Your day's done. We're meeting Olesk back at the garage." He leaned forward with a business card between his fingers. She took it and put it in her jacket without looking. Grant asked, "You ever hear of the Seventh Syndicate?"

"I have," she responded evenly. They were the bastards she wanted.

"When you outgrow Olesk, which should be soon..." Grant sat back and spread his arms out along the top edge of the seat. "Give me a call for some real work."

She patted her pocket and saluted him with a nod. "Thank you." He smiled with self-satisfaction and stared out into the city night as they pulled out of the parking lot. But she knew he wouldn't be grinning smugly if he knew the stolen cell phone was in her other pocket, and that she was one step closer to lighting the fuse.

Chapter Eleven

They were losing their light and Arash was losing his patience. After finalizing the cages for human cargo in the vans, they'd moved on to modifying the engines. The excitement and satisfaction he usually felt while upgrading a car was completely bleached away by the intent behind these builds. Hector, Thom and Ellie didn't seem to care, and it was insane. Every time Arash had to go inside the vans, or even look into the cargo area, he imagined the terror of whoever was going to be trapped in there.

Marcos's conscience got him killed. Arash suppressed his disgust and anger to act like he was just in it for the money. But by doing that, he was only building pressure inside himself, and he knew he would crack.

He installed an aftermarket air intake kit on one of the vans while Hector and Thom wrapped up their work doing the same on the other. The sun split the clouds for one minute of relief, then fell behind the mountains. A whole day had passed and Stephanie hadn't returned. Not knowing where she was or what was happening with her amplified his edginess. Ellie hadn't relayed any information. It was as if Stephanie had never existed. He kept eyeing the cars and motorcycles scattered around the compound. Any of them could speed him into the city to search for her. But Arash was trapped in the growing darkness, as if it was him chained to the bench seat in the van. His work light cast hard shadows, making him shift constantly to inspect his work.

Ellie was a good enough manager to understand the conditions. She walked from the house toward Arash and the others with four beers in her hand. "Wrap it up," she called out. "We'll get back at it tomorrow."

Instead of walking to her, Hector angled at the van Arash was working on. "Let me see that job."

"You're not my supervisor." Arash released the hood support and slammed the hood down before Hector could get close enough to see. Arash leaned on the front of the van to emphasize that Hector would not get what he wanted.

"I have seniority." Hector puffed up and Thom backed him.

Thom toed open a cardboard box next to Arash's van and peered at the contents before exclaiming, "He's not even as far along as we are. This isn't hard work, man, it's all the same fittings."

Arash didn't budge for the two men. "Shut the hell up and twitch, Thom. And don't you ever question my work, Hector. I've been wrenching since you were eating breakfast cereal." Hector's head tilted to the side and his mouth turned down in a scowl. He was ready to fight. Arash pressed because it was the worst idea and he was too damn trapped. "Oh, wait. That's still happening now."

Hector drew his fists back to charge Arash and Ellie slid between them, beers raised high. "Bloody hell. Drink beer. Calm down." But she didn't have the mass or leverage to stop Hector and he barreled into her. The beers went flying and she spun down to her knees.

Hector's momentum carried him into Arash with a bone-shaking impact. Arash braced his legs and started to swivel to get Hector off him, but Thom jumped in, fists flying. One punch caught Arash on his chest, just next to his shoulder, and the muscle seized. Before Thom could get another blow in, Arash swung Hector into the path of the strike. Thom punched Hector in the temple and Hector yelled his pain into Arash's ear.

Arash drove a knee into Hector's side while he was off balance, making him wheeze and clutch at Arash's shoulders to stay upright. Thom cradled his knuckles after striking Hector and wasn't paying attention to how close he still was to the action. Arash reached past Hector, wrapped his hand around the back of Thom's neck and yanked him forward. Thom's face smashed into Hector's skull and both men wobbled, dazed. Arash twisted out of Hector's grip and let him fall to the dirt with Thom next to him.

Ellie scrambled away from them and stood. "Bloody wankers." She dusted off her jeans.

"And now you know what it's like to question me." Arash blazed with fury. He could finish both men right now. With his knife, or a heavy tool from the jobsite. These people killed Marcos. But Olesk was the head. Making Hector and Thom pay would be the end of Arash's stay with the STR. He had to wait to get them all.

Thom and Hector struggled to their feet and leaned on each other for support. Each man squeezed his eyes shut and opened them wide, trying to focus. Ellie spoke through clenched teeth. "Enough. Not one more inch, you idiots. If you throw this gig off by one second, you are dead. We are all dead." She speared her finger toward the house. "Go inside and drink your beers."

Hector and Thom tried to glare at Arash, but the haze in their eyes undermined any attempt at intimidation. And then there was the fact that they propped each other up like a couple of drunks while Arash stood on his own two legs. He stared back at them and didn't even need to move to make them turn and shuffle toward the house. Arash didn't follow. When Ellie questioned him with a look, he tipped his head at a collection of different types of motorcycles next to one of the barns. "Are those for riding?"

"Anything but the street bikes." She waved him toward the machines. "If it runs, take it."

He turned his back to the others and walked to the bikes. There were at least two hundred yards of decent dirt behind the house before the hills got too steep and a wire fence demarcated the edge of civilization.

Arash found a dual-purpose motorcycle with air in the tires and swung his leg over it. After two kicks on the starter, he got the engine cranking to a high whine. Twisting the throttle blew carbon out of the tailpipe. He snapped it into gear and let the clutch go. The engine had enough power to jump him away from the other bikes and toward the open field.

Hector and the others stood where he'd left them, watching. Arash pushed the bike faster. The dim headlight only gave him a few feet of rushing ground before him, making him concentrate hard on the ride. Any distractions and he'd be eating dirt without a helmet. After a few seconds he nearly ran into the wire fence and swerved at the last moment. Dust billowed, tasting dry and mineral. He needed a beer to cool down, but he got more of a rush from twisting the throttle again and speeding along the edge of the fence.

The motorcycle was game, if a little loose in the suspension. He fishtailed in softer soil, his pulse racing as high as the engine. With a little extra speed, he could jump the fence and leave all these psychopaths behind. But running now would haunt him forever, the same way seeing Marcos's blood mixed with the fluids from the car wreck persisted in his memory.

Another fence jutted down from the one he rode along. He'd reached the far edge of the property and skidded to a stop. Looking down, he saw that Ellie and the others had gone inside. Beyond the house was the main road. It knifed into the suburbs, then disappeared on its way to the glowing city in the distance. No cars lit it up now. Stephanie was out there somewhere. Hopefully alive. He couldn't take another ghost begging him for revenge.

STEPHANIE LOVED TO DRIVE, but she was more than happy to be in the passenger seat while Olesk took them back to the compound. Grant hadn't talked to her at all after handing over his card. In the parking lot, he and Olesk had exchanged some words alone before Grant got behind the wheel of his car and pulled away. She'd taken her time alone to secretly turn the volume all the way down on her stolen phone. All Olesk relayed when he waved her to his car was that Grant was complimentary of her work.

After that, Olesk was his usual driving machine. She decompressed to the base level of tension and danger that had been established when she joined up with the STR. Asking casual questions about the progress with the vans resulted in nonanswers from Olesk. He said he'd been taking care of business in town and hadn't been back to the compound all day. Worry ramped up in her as she thought of Arash being outnumbered. Olesk's tone while driving was always so flat there could be good news or disaster waiting for them.

The glow of the city swept past. The suburbs were quiet. Beyond them, the dark hills tumbled closer. Olesk spoke, and she couldn't tell if it was for her, or to himself. "The Slick Track Racers started as a bunch of idiot teenagers getting faster than the suburbs on a slick track that's now a home store next to a chain sports bar next to a pet supply store. We got really good. We started to get hired on the real streets. But only the best survived. That was me." His expression remained stony. "I built this gang to handle anything anyone threw at us. You've got wheels, and I like it."

That was it. He clammed up and drove, constantly in

motion but not paying her any attention. Tiny lights in the distance revealed where the houses nestled in the wild. She looked ahead, trying to identify which one was the compound. As if she'd be able to tell what she was racing toward.

There were no smouldering craters or burning structures. Olesk turned up the drive and she saw the house was intact. The front door opened when he parked and Ellie came down the steps to greet him. As soon as he stepped from the car, his demeanor transformed to a comfortable man, in control. He met Ellie with a quick kiss to her lips, then proceeded to the house.

Ellie continued to Stephanie with an envelope in her outstretched hand. "Job well-done, from what I heard."

Stephanie took the envelope and looked over another eight-thousand-dollar payday. "Did you expect anything other than perfection?"

"Absolutely not." Ellie smiled at her. A motorcycle engine grated high from behind the house. Ellie tipped her head that way. "I think he missed you." Ellie skipped off after Olesk.

The mechanical sound grew louder. A dark rider burst into the glow from the house, a cloud of dust behind him. Arash rocketed closer and put his foot down to skid in a hard turn toward Stephanie. He gunned the engine and sped to her side. His intense eyes devoured her. His voice was just loud enough over the sound of the engine. "You good?"

"I'm good." This close to him she felt her breath rushing. Her relief at seeing him was overcome by a deeper need to be pressed against his body. "You good?"

"Now I am." He nodded, mouth severe. The man looked wild, near a breaking point. He revved the engine. "Want to go for a ride?"

Either she growled, or it was the motor resonating in her chest. "Get us out of here." She swung her leg over the back of the bike and snugged herself up against Arash's back. The complications of who he was and what he was doing with this gang tried to hook into her and drag her away, but the heated contact was too powerful. It felt so real, his strong body and sure posture. She damned the consequences and convinced herself she would deal with them later. For now, she reveled in the feel of his hips against the insides of her thighs.

"Go," she urged him.

The bike lurched, forcing her to wrap herself tighter around Arash. He firmed where she touched him. They took off and sped past the house. The dual-purpose motorcycle wasn't sprung for two people, making for a rough ride. But that just made her and Arash find a common balance, both of them in the moment. He took them over the dirt lot behind the house. Darkness rushed past, and for a moment it seemed like they could fly into the black hills ahead. She breathed as if her lungs were as large as those mysteries, as if all the burdens of the day and this mission didn't bear down on her. As if she was kissing Arash in freedom.

He skidded to a stop and she saw the wire fence that hemmed them in. There was no freedom. The engine idled low. She followed Arash's gaze back down to the house and barns. The two white vans were parked next to a barn, boxes and tools spread out around them. The dim headlight of the motorcycle just illuminated the darkness in Arash's eyes.

He asked, "Do you know what the gig is?"

"I don't." She did, but not through Olesk, so she couldn't blow her cover.

"Does it matter to you?" Doubt stained his voice.

"Cash will only pay for so much." At first she thought he might be testing her loyalty to the STR, but he'd already revealed too much of his own concern.

His wary glance took in the house, then turned to her, dead serious. "We're building rolling cages. For people."

She didn't think her heart could beat any faster, but this flash of conscience from Arash made it thunder. He didn't belong here. She might have an ally. The connection she'd felt with him became more real.

She brought her mouth close to his ear. "Give me twenty minutes, then we're going to get off this compound for some privacy."

He nodded, caution returning to his eyes. She gathered herself against him again and he took off back toward the house. The man in her arms hadn't changed; she'd just learned more of him. But instead of explaining him, this new information only deepened his mystery.

Back at the house, she dismounted near the rear door. He rocked the bike side to side to hear the gasoline slosh in the tank. "There's a little fuel left." He checked his watch, held her eyes for a moment, then tore back into the darkness.

She marked the time and headed inside. The kitchen was empty as she passed through. Video game sounds and small conversation echoed out of one of the living rooms, but no one paid her any attention when she climbed the stairs. After a visit to the bathroom, she closed herself in her room and wedged the door with the buckle of her bag's strap.

Sitting on the floor with her back propped on the wall, she allowed her body to relax in increments. Once she was sure she hadn't been followed upstairs, she took out the stolen phone and brought up the lock screen. Football Jersey was probably at the hospital getting his wrist x-rayed and wrapped in a cast, so he didn't have time to search the parking lot for his phone or have the account canceled. Gauging the mentality of the man she took it from, the first code she tried was 6969. It didn't work. She guessed his age was somewhere in the twenties, meaning his birth year would be in the nineties. Before she started with that run, she keyed in the largest number associated with the parking lot harasser, the jersey number. 7575. The phone unlocked.

Urgency straightened her posture. She muted all the sounds from the phone, opened the web browser and navigated to the fan fiction message board Frontier Justice used to communicate. Narrowing down to the relevant thread, she quickly typed about a fictional story line for a TV show that takes the characters to Reno. She listed all the addresses she remembered, but offset all the numbers by four, so any paranoid web searches by the Seventh Syndicate wouldn't bring people to this site. Cars were described, as well as people, but she couldn't use names in this format.

When she'd texted Ty and Vincent with the burner phone, she'd given them Arash's first name and her belief that he was a mechanic at some point. A comment on this thread referred to The Mechanic and explained that he had no criminal record. That fit with the Arash she knew. But it didn't explain what the hell he was doing with Olesk.

She closed the web browser and cleared out the cache and history. The phone was a different model from hers and she didn't have a charger for it. The battery was down to 25 percent. Football Jersey might cancel it before that, so she had to assume that this resource was closed off to her now.

But she might not be completely isolated in her mission. She pocketed the phone and gathered herself before stepping out of her room and back downstairs. Arash stood at the edge of the living room with his back to the wall. The dust of the land colored his chest and shoulders. His windswept hair accentuated his wary eyes. Like he'd ventured down to civilization from the dark hills. Just for Stephanie, from the way he heated when he gazed at her.

Olesk sat alone with his phone at his table while Ellie and Hector played video games and Thom paced while watching. Stephanie stated to no one in particular, "Rubber chicken isn't going to do it for me tonight."

Thom kept pacing, his gaze on the video game. A dark bruise ringed one of his eyes. Olesk pointed vaguely south. "There's a supermarket three miles down the road. I don't want anyone dining out and giving too much face."

Ellic paused the game and Hector exclaimed, "I was winning!"

"We need more beer and frozen egg rolls." She reached into her pocket and peeled off a few hundred-dollar bills.

"Keys to the gunmetal gray minivan out front?" Stephanie stepped forward and took the money.

"On the rack of hooks in the garage." Olesk still stared at his phone. "Go easy. It's working in the next gig and still needs to be dialed in."

She waved, though no one saw it, and moved to Arash. The game resumed, its noise walling off the others and making her voice more intimate than she'd anticipated. "Steak and onions?"

"I'll cook it." He remained cagey, though the draw between them was palpable.

"Come with me, pick out your ingredients."

When he stepped away from the wall it was like they were the only two people on earth. His nearness seared her and she had to know how deep the burn would go. Then he somehow restrained himself, and that's when she saw just how strong-willed he was. Because the intensity he showed could level this whole house. She wanted to wreck it all with him.

But there were still too many questions. She took a half step backward and the electricity between them reduced to the usual constant crackling hum. The two of them found the inside door to the garage, where there were three more cars, one of them not much more than a frame with wheels. Boxes of power tools, some unopened, were stacked in a corner next to shelves filled with home electronics of all varieties.

Arash looked over a rack of hooks by the door and selected the only ones that could be for the minivan. "You want the wheel?" he asked.

"Take it. I was driving all day."

Cold night knifed down once they walked out the front of the house. They hurried to the minivan and jumped in. Arash turned the starter and the motor juddered. She felt the powerful torque of the modified engine but knew it wasn't running as optimally as it could. From the way Arash hovered his hands over the steering wheel, head cocked listening, she sensed he felt it, too. "Timing," he declared.

"It's wheezing. Air/fuel mix is off."

"Main computer needs to be updated for the mods they made." He put it into Drive and paused again as the car strained against the brakes. "We've got work to do." The minivan kicked dirt behind it before grabbing hold and jumping forward.

She hoped he was right, that they could truly work together. That he was the man she thought he was. It was a chance she had to take. She headed into the night with the dark mystery that was Arash. The only light was the flame of a fuse she just set. If she and Arash were both fighting on the same side, the blast could crack the foundation of Olesk and the Seventh. If she was wrong about him, she could be dead by the end of the night.

Chapter Twelve

The minivan was a mechanical mess. Exactly how Arash felt inside. Nothing meshed, the potential was hindered and it felt like any minute all the bolts would come loose and he would wreck into the dark asphalt. Stephanie rode calmly next to him, but he knew she held a secret. Something was coming.

They reached the supermarket and stepped into the parking lot like an ordinary couple buying groceries for the family. The other shoppers had no idea that he'd been building cages in vans, because if they had, they'd have been pointing and howling at the monster he'd become.

But he and Stephanie cruised easily into the produce section, their cart leading the way. She asked casually, "Did you give Thom that bruise?"

"He and Hector kept talking when they should've shut up. They started swinging when they should've known better."

"You alright?" Actual concern showed in her eyes and it threw him further off balance.

"Nothing a steak won't fix." He stretched his chest until the bruise caught.

"Good. You have to be careful with them."

"Those little brats have to be careful with me." He collected onions and peppers while she wandered an aisle away. Was she just building his trust to get him to lower his guard?

She approached him with a question in her eyes and he braced himself. "Allergies? Preferences?" She dropped a bagged head of lettuce in the cart.

"No uncooked mushrooms," he told her. She couldn't have wanted to get him alone to talk about salads.

"Me, neither." She wrinkled her nose. "Too squeaky." Then she was gone again, gathering vegetables. He pressed on, finding more of what he needed for a simple meal. When she returned with more food, the inquisitive look remained on her face. "When did you start wrenching?"

"Eight or nine years old." This story couldn't come back to burn him if Olesk found out. Arash's friendship with Marcos started in high school. "We had a neighbor in the apartment complex who was a mechanic for the public bus. I'd hang out with him after school while he was massaging his Camaro."

"Your parents weren't your gateway?" Her attention remained on him instead of the shopping.

There hadn't been any shame in his profession from them, but he could never talk shop with his father. "They were lawyers in Iran before they fled, but my dad wound up with restaurant and delivery work. My mom was a secretary for these Persian real estate guys. They both worked a ton so we could get by." He and Stephanie reached the spice aisle and he threw some jars in the cart.

"Are they still around?"

He couldn't let too much information wind up hurting his folks. "Yeah, they're good," was all he'd say.

She stopped walking and her face grew serious. It felt like the silence before an earthquake. She spoke in a quiet voice. "You don't belong in Olesk's gang."

A chill shot down to his bones. He knew they hadn't been followed on the road to the market, but someone could already be waiting for him here. There was one exit in the front, but he might be able to get into the service areas, then out through the loading dock. Sickening acid burned with the thought that all of this with Stephanie, the kiss, the need to get him alone, had all been a setup to find him out. Then kill him.

She stood so calm. Was this how it came? Without a blink from her. But he wasn't ready to tear open his shirt and give her his heart to stab.

"You're just as new as me. You don't get to make that call." He shifted the cart that was between them.

She'd picked the perfect place to confront him. With the public watching, they couldn't get too loud and he couldn't get physical defending himself until he was absolutely sure she was coming at him. Her demeanor remained cool. Anyone watching would think they were just a couple with a domestic disagreement. But he knew this was a minefield of life or death. She held his gaze calmly. "I don't belong, either."

"You're smart. You knew what you were getting into." He wanted so much to believe her, but that was what she'd been using against him all along.

"I knew *exactly* what I was getting into." She came around to his side of the cart but kept her hands on the edge where he could see them. "But I don't think you did."

It didn't come out as a threat, but he still watched over her shoulder for anyone else gunning for him. Everything seemed ordinary. All of that could change in a second. He angled so he could hold her off with one arm while reaching for his knife with his other hand if he had to. "You've got me all figured out."

"I don't." She assessed his posture and took a step back, hands spread in a truce. "I can't figure out what you're doing with Olesk."

This day had played out in agonies, and it wasn't over.

Not long ago, he'd thought she was gone forever, then this woman was wrapped around him, getting as free as they could on the motorcycle. And now she was one step away from signing his death sentence. "Same as you." How far would this go? "It's green and shaped like money."

"I think you're lying." So steady, like a scalpel over his heart. He probably wouldn't feel it when she came in for the kill. More emotion slipped into her voice. "There isn't enough cash in the world to clear your conscience from those cages you built."

Conscience. The same word Olesk had used. The same impulse that had gotten Marcos killed. It might just get Arash killed. Tonight. At the hands of the woman he wanted to trust. "You have no idea what I'm capable of."

"You're capable of caring." She stepped forward again, warmth in her eyes. "More than anyone in Olesk's gang."

"Including you?" He hadn't been able to account for her ethic before and now he was completely twisted without a compass.

Her voice dropped. "I'm not in Olesk's gang." She slid closer. "Do you know about the Seventh Syndicate?"

Those killers wouldn't hesitate to assassinate someone in public. Every face in the crowd was suddenly a menace, coming to get him. Including Stephanie. How could she be part of that criminal organization? They were the worst of the worst. "I do." He spoke through clenched teeth, prepared for the bullet through his flesh and the fight to get out.

"They're the client. I was driving one of them around all day." She curled her hand into a fist. "They're the ones you built the cage for." His mind spun to keep up with all the transitions she steered him through. Her eyes blazed. "The gig is human trafficking. They're collecting boys and girls and selling them. Homeless. Runaways. Asylum seekers. People the system is failing to protect. I'm here to stop it. And I don't want to hurt you when I do."

He moved so close he only had to whisper. "You're a cop?"

"God, no." The wry smile he'd gotten to know returned to her lips for a second, then was gone. She subtlety checked around them, then said, "I'm part of a very unofficial organization. We move in when the law can't. We're called Frontier Justice."

"Never heard of it." He couldn't figure out if this bizarre new information was part of an ongoing test.

"It's new." She tipped her head from side to side and corrected, "It's old. Started over a hundred and fifty years ago by my ancestor and others out West. Immigrants and women and former slaves and anyone who the law wouldn't protect. We stepped in then, and we're doing it again."

"You think you can take on the Seventh?" She seemed so confident with this truth, but then again, she'd convinced Olesk she was a car thief.

"We already have." A few more people moved into the produce area of the store and she pushed the cart away, Arash at her side. "Did you hear about a shootout at an apple orchard on the Monterey Bay? Or one at a mansion down in San Jose? That was us, running the Seventh off."

The shooting in San Jose had made the news, but they'd only said it was related to organized crime. No mention of vigilante groups riding out of the Old West. "But not completely off." Not if they were the ones behind the big gig Olesk was prepping for.

"That'll take time." She stopped them midway down an empty aisle. "It'll take operations like the one I'm on now."

"You're taking a big risk telling me." It was starting to make sense, but maybe it all fit too well, like a perfect fabrication.

"You're worth it." The electric connection between them crackled again. "I see you. Your heart, your mind. A man who helps a stranger with her car in a parking lot isn't supposed to build cages for human trafficking. You're going to get hurt with Olesk's gang, and you don't deserve it. You don't belong with them."

They were still alone in the aisle. He moved to her and voiced words he hadn't said to anyone else. "I'm with them to kill them."

A stillness descended. She stared at him, into him, lips parted with shock. "Explain."

"At least I can surprise you, too." He smiled. Lifting the lies allowed fresh blood to flow through him.

A small laugh bubbled up in her. "You always do." Her eyes remained sharp, searching him.

Arash discovered the words. "I had a friend who ran with the STR for a minute. Then he found out what the next gig was all about. He wanted to get out. He called me. They murdered him on the highway."

"I'm sorry." Real emotion showed on her face, and he saw that his new knowledge of her didn't change her that much.

"Thank you." He was hit with the urge to reach forward and touch her arm, but there was still too much to sort. "But you should be sorry for Olesk and the STR. They're the ones going down in flames."

"We can help each other." A clever smile crossed her lips and shined dark in her eyes.

His first instinct to mistrust battled against all the trust she'd just given him. Her life was in his hands as much as his was in hers. Either could out the other to Olesk, and then it would all be over. He'd already grown to think of her as his only tentative ally in this whole mess. And now it made sense why. "I can see that." But what her and her organization wanted was still hazy. "But you can't stop me from taking Olesk."

"He's yours," she said. "I'm here for the Seventh Syndicate." Her mouth turned down when she said their name. "There are Frontier Justice people in the police, the FBI.

We can use those resources now, and when the time comes, their authority can lock these bastards up."

"If there's anything left of them."

"Then we *can* help each other."

"What you told me about learning the cars, about private school and all that, was it all true?" The electric charge snapped between them. Trying to understand Stephanie was like falling through an endless maze.

"All true." She nodded. "The only thing I lied about to you was why I was in this gang."

"When you told me to kiss you?" His heart beat faster. He wanted to believe her, but he held himself back from bringing his hands to her waist and drawing her to him.

She glanced at his mouth, then gazed in his eyes. "All true."

"When you pushed me away?" There was no map with her.

"That's when I thought you were a criminal." She reached forward and took his hand in hers. A steady current moved through him with the touch. Stronger than before. She wasn't part of the gang. She was on his side.

"I'm a mechanic." With a vow to a dead friend.

Her hold of him grew stronger. He pulled her toward him. They met, chest to chest, and wrapped their arms around each other. The fear and danger he'd been living in hadn't gone away. But knowing she was there with him, a woman as capable as she was, made the most dire situation seem possible. He could live through this. And he had to, in order to discover what this electricity was when he was so close to Stephanie.

She tilted her face to his and he took her mouth with a kiss. It felt as if they were both sighing relief into each other. The lies were gone, and the truth made them stronger together. Her lips slid against his. He opened his mouth and she met him with the same hunger.

A footstep into the aisle broke them apart. The two of them smiled sheepishly at an older white woman who pushed her cart past and pretended not to look at them. But he didn't feel sheepish. He felt bold, because what he had with Stephanie was powerful enough to take down Olesk and anyone around him.

Stephanie arranged the edges of her hair and pulled out a cell phone from her jacket. It was different from the one he'd seen her with. "You a big football fan?" he asked. The phone's well-worn case had a large team logo on it.

She pushed the cart away from the other shopper with her elbows while unlocking the phone. "Stole it from a fan who wanted a lap dance in a parking lot this evening."

"What?" Anger fired through his muscles.

Her voice remained low. "I had to steal it. It's the only way I can get word out to my team without leaving a trail."

"I don't care about you stealing. What about the guy who was hassling you?"

"Him and two others." She waved it off.

"Are you kidding?" He'd known it was going to be trouble when Olesk took her off that morning. The thought of three sons of bitches coming at her nearly blinded him with rage. "Are you okay?"

"I am." She moved the cart to another aisle and stopped. "Thank you. Really." Warmth shimmered in the depth of her eyes. "Barely a scratch." She slid her hand down Arash's arm. "And the guy who gave me this phone is going to be at least six weeks in a cast."

"That's not bad enough." He knew she could handle herself, and hated that she had to.

She squeezed his forearm, expression brightening. "His wrist will probably need pins."

"That's better." But he still wanted to release his own anger on those guys.

"And I got a phone out of it." She swiped over the screen

and opened the web browser. "I'm going to contact my team and catch them up."

And suddenly he was less alone in this darkness than he ever thought. "Okay. Look bored. I'll go get the beer." She nodded and he headed up the aisle. Glancing back before turning into the rest of the store, he saw she'd taken on the perfect relaxed posture of a woman on her phone without a concern about the world around her. Everyone in the store believed it. Except him. They were both living on the outside. Lying to the world. Lying to Olesk.

He returned with the beer to find her another aisle over, shopping casually. The phone had been put away. She smiled when he approached. It was real, for him and not for show. He knew it because the same surprise bloomed in his chest when he saw her.

They continued shopping, talking only about the food as thousands of questions raced through him. As they selected cooking pots and pans he picked the first question. "Did you really steal that Mercedes?"

"The whole process was legit." A small and wicked smile shined like a knife. "But it was my car."

"You're bad." He knew he'd never be able to keep up with the webs she wove.

"I haven't always been good." The smile faded.

"Neither have I," he confessed.

They fell silent among the people in line for the register. As they edged closer to the conveyor belt a hot rod magazine cover caught their attention. Talking about paint finishes and carburetor modifications kept them occupied. But it didn't bring him back to the real world. There was no real world he recognized anymore. Not when they paid for the groceries with cash blood money from Olesk's gang. Not when, as soon as they got outside the supermarket, Stephanie disabled the stolen cell phone, twisted it until it cracked and threw it in the trash.

Not when she leaned into his body as they approached the minivan and whispered, "It might be bugged."

He nodded, his cheek against her temple. This was real. The only trust in this deadly landscape was between them. He never counted on someone helping him, but Stephanie was way beyond anything he could've imagined. They had people to protect and vengeance to pay. And he would fight like hell for her.

Chapter Thirteen

The dark of night was hers now. Stephanie had risked it all with Arash, confronting him the way she had, and the gamble had paid off with a bigger reward than she'd ever imagined. She had an ally in the fight. A partner driving her through the black hills on the return to the compound. That space approached with less foreboding. She had entered into this mission wrapped in secrets. She brought more with her now. Arash made her stronger.

For a minute at the supermarket, she thought it would all blow up in her face. Of course he wouldn't confess right away to her. She hadn't been completely forthcoming herself. But once their trust extended and met in the middle like a bridge, they were able to cross.

She watched him now, driving the disjointed minivan through the night. He focused forward, jaw set. So much made sense now. She'd been right; he didn't fit. But his reason caught her completely off guard. His purpose and dedication to his fallen friend illuminated some of the depths she'd seen in him. She wanted to learn more, but the car could be listening, and they were fast approaching the compound.

To communicate, she extended her hand toward him. He didn't hesitate to reach out and lace his fingers through hers. They'd been keeping secrets and hiding truths, and all through it, this was real. The touch burned with a steady warmth.

And it brought its own complications. Her initial hope in confronting him was to get him out of the gang so he wouldn't get caught up in the firestorm she and Frontier Justice were planning. But Arash had his own mission, promised with blood, and she could see he wouldn't quit until it was complete. Which meant her stakes just went up. Because while it was amazing to know he had her back, she also knew that she would be devastated if anything happened to Arash.

He let go of her hand and steered them off the main road. The lights of Olesk's house turned the cars and motorcycles out front into hulking silhouettes. Sleeping monsters a moment away from waking and killing.

Beer bottles clinked in their cases as the minivan rocked over the uneven dirt of the driveway. Ellie could probably hear that sound from three hundred yards away during a hailstorm. She was out the front door before Arash had shut the engine down. Ellie threw the minivan's side door back and hefted a stack of two cases of beers. A knowing smile grew when she watched Arash and Stephanie stand close to collect more of the groceries. Stephanie met her gaze with a smile of her own. There were a lot of buried secrets, some explosive enough to kill, but Stephanie didn't have to pretend this was anything other than it was.

"How does it ride?" Ellie asked, lifting her eyebrows with a little growl.

Arash must not have seen her suggestive expression and answered honestly. "Rolls too much in the turns, needs to be tightened down."

"Well, I'm sure you can get it tight." Ellie shot Stephanie one last glance, then carried the beers to the house.

Arash closed the door to the van and stood next to Stephanie with the bags of food in his hands. "Am I that obvious?"

"Ashamed to be seen with me?" It wasn't fair to needle him too hard. She was willing to let Olesk's gang think all they wanted to about her and Arash, but she hadn't mentioned anything about the attraction or the intensity of the kissing to her own team.

"Hell, no."

"Then put some swagger into it." She bumped her hip against his.

"Oh, I can swagger." And he proved it as he strutted to the house, giving her an excellent view of the sway of his body.

"That's the way I like it." She remained close, caught up in his carnal currents.

Inside the house, Ellie had already unboxed the beers and lined them up in the refrigerator. Four fresh ones waited on the counter. Hector and Thom wandered into the kitchen and watched, but didn't help, as Arash and Stephanie unpacked the food.

Hector picked up the packaged steak and looked it over. "What're you going to cook me?"

Arash tossed a box of frozen food onto the island in front of him. "She's the only one who placed an order." The two men glared at each other.

"I'm not feeling that hungry." Thom pulled a bag of lettuce toward him. "I'll just have a salad."

"Not mine." Stephanie pinned the lettuce to the island with her hand.

Thom straightened and jutted his jaw. "You guys just aren't team players."

She faced him. "I'm not part of this team to be your mother or your cook. I can drive and I can fight. And if you need proof of either, keep talking."

Thom licked his moving, silent lips. He stared at her, bruise ringing one eye, and looked up and over her shoulder, where she knew Arash was standing. Menacing energy radiated behind her. Hector broke the tension by grabbing one of the beers and sliding it over to Thom before giving him a hard slap on the back. "You don't even eat salad, bro." Thom still didn't move, so Hector lifted the beer and placed it in his chest so Thom had to grab it. Hector took his own beer and led the way out of the room. Thom reluctantly followed.

Ellie took up the two remaining beers. "I wish you two would go easy on Thom. He's twitchy."

"If he doesn't want to dance, he has to stay off the floor." Stephanie resumed putting the food away.

Ellie shrugged to Stephanie and Arash. "Please don't break any fingers so he can still work on the cars."

Arash growled behind her. "No promises."

"Ah." Ellie put the beers down. "Change and receipt." Stephanie pulled both from her jacket and handed them over. "Cheers." Ellie toasted with one of the beers, drank and started out of the kitchen.

Olesk met her at the border of the other rooms and took the other beer from her. He casually looked over the food Arash was laying out for tonight's dinner. "Tomorrow," Olesk said, "Arash is completing his work on the cargo van's engine. Stephanie, you're on to the minivan you were driving tonight. When Arash is done, he's on the minivan with you."

"I like it," Stephanie answered.

"Sounds good." Arash nodded to Olesk and arranged a pan on the stove.

"That minivan…" Olesk stared into the distance and she recognized the focus he had when he drove. "It's our secret stealth rocket. I don't want anyone to look at it and know it's a beast. And I don't want anyone to be able to catch it."

"I've got plans for it." Arash grinned.

She added, "It'll be a bullet."

Olesk's attention came back to the room. "Boom." He smiled, drank from his beer and left with Ellie.

Even alone, Stephanie and Arash couldn't speak. The glance they shared after Olesk's departure said enough. Arash clearly didn't like the man, and now she understood what had been behind his hair trigger with the gang. He'd played it well, though, pushing just enough to show he had a mind of his own, but still getting his work done and not alienating himself. That internal tension was mirrored in her own.

"I still haven't seen your knife work." Arash placed an onion and a cutting board on the island.

"One of those guys in the parking lot almost found out." She unwrapped a cooking knife they'd bought at the supermarket and tested the moderate edge against her thumb.

Arash took out another new knife and slapped the steaks down on a cutting board. "Wish I'd been there." He wasn't particularly delicate cutting the excess fat off the steaks.

"To see the show?" She flipped the knife in the air and caught it by the handle. The conflict was easy to brush off after taking out the men, but Arash's heated response resonated unexpectedly through her. She mattered to him.

"To bust their heads." He set the knife down and looked at her. "I know you can handle yourself. No doubt at all. But… I wish you hadn't had to."

Every word lit fires deep in her chest. "Thank you." The video game in the other room prompted taunting shouts that broke the moment between Stephanie and Arash. She took up her knife and sliced the onion. He finished with the steak and prepped the pan at the stove. While he worked she put the rest of the vegetables together.

Onions hit the oil in the pan and for a moment it seemed like an ordinary house. A hot meal, freshly cooked. Two people moving about a kitchen with ease, checking in with each other about how they liked their food.

Never mind the gun on her belt, the knife in her pocket or the blood money from the day's job in her jacket. Or Arash's thirst for revenge against the very people who welcomed them under this roof. Or the cages that had been built into the vans.

She couldn't forget any of that, but she could allow herself to find comfort in the moment as she watched Arash push the onions to the edge of the pan and lay the steaks in. They sizzled and spattered and filled the space with aromas more real than any of the frozen dinners.

Arash was real, too. Connecting with him had reminded her that she wasn't just an operative with Frontier Justice— she was a person.

She remembered her earlier purchase. "I've got dessert." But when she pulled out the packages of cookies from the empanada restaurant from her coat, she found they'd all been crushed. "Those jerks in the parking lot." It must've happened in the thick of the fight.

Arash looked at the mess of cookies within the cellophane wrappers. "I didn't think I could hate those guys even more." He finished cooking and they took their food to the table in the kitchen and sat next to each other so they both had their backs to the wall.

She savored the first bite of food. Arash chewed and nodded. Her shoulder brushed against his and the two of them were uncomplicated humans for a few heartbeats. The meal continued, as did the conversations in the other room. If she and Arash had any privacy, she could ask him about his friend's involvement in the gang, and if Arash had a specific plan for taking them down. A hundred other questions. She was sure he had plenty. Instead she stuck to what would look best to the others. "Can you reprogram the brain on the minivan?"

He took a pull from a bottle of water. "As long as we

have a scanner and a laptop with the right software, no problem. I bet you could, too."

"I have a little experience with it." But all of her equipment was in her condo. "Still have to dial in the shocks, get the timing right."

"It'll be a job." He drummed his fingers on the table. "We can probably strip some weight from the interior without it looking modified."

"I can't wait to get in there with you." If only it was just the two of them wrenching on a car for the love of the grease.

"We'll be so good." He toasted her water with his. They drank and she understood he was doing the same centering that she had to. Amid all these criminals and their bad intentions, what she and Arash were doing was right.

THE MAZE HE walked was just as deadly, but having Stephanie with him seemed to brighten the blind corners. The path, still twisted, seemed clearer ahead. They'd finished their dinner talking about the modifications to the minivan. To the rest of the STR, it looked like a romance; the real intentions remained hidden. Not that the connection between him and Stephanie wasn't real.

Climbing the stairs at the end of the day had been torture. His body raged for her, but his mind knew that there was no safety for that kind of contact. They didn't even kiss, but the look they shared before parting to their rooms was heavy with the need they both shared, and it kept him warm through the night on his lonely mattress on the floor.

He woke wondering if all of her unbelievable revelations had been a dream. It seemed like the best way to explain a secret vigilante group started by her ancestor sometime back in the 1800s. But when he caught her eye downstairs, fixing her breakfast, he knew it was all real. She was more complicated with mysteries than he'd ever imagined.

Everyone got to work quickly that morning. The damp chill outside had wilted the cardboard boxes for the auto parts, but he heated up as soon as he started wrenching. Stephanie drove the minivan behind the house and started to assess the modifications. Soon there was an extensive list written in her tidy script on a whiteboard next to the minivan.

Hector and Thom had finished modifying the engine on their cargo van and were now elbows deep in boxes of electronics and wiring. This aspect of the build hadn't been discussed, and every detail could mean life or death for him and Stephanie. Arash leaned out from behind his open hood to call out to them. "Both vans getting that?"

"Yeah," Thom grumbled, hands busy untangling wires.

"Alright. Two minutes and this one's all yours." Arash couldn't see what they were working on.

Stephanie joined in. "Do I need to add that to the list for the minivan?"

"No." Hector shook his head. "Just the two vans are getting the coms." Hector held up a handheld mic on a coiled cable, like the kind from a police car radio.

"Got it." Stephanie nodded to Hector and shot a quick glance to Arash before returning to her business.

A motor growled to life at the front of the house. Moments later Olesk drove a sport-tuned Subaru around back, with Ellie walking at its side. They parked and Olesk popped open the hood. He spoke while staring down into the engine. "Cargo vans and the Subaru have the coms. Minivan has to look stock. They'll get their updates through the phone."

Arash secured the last bolt on the air intake modification and waved Hector toward the cargo van. "Do your worst." Hector collected a couple of boxes of electronics and carried them to the van. Arash gathered some tools and joined Stephanie at the minivan. "Private school handwriting." He looked over the list on the whiteboard.

"I speak French, too." She reached into the minivan's engine and tested the clamps on a radiator hose. He would've liked to just stand there and watch as she tightened everything down, but instead he walked over to Olesk.

"You have a laptop and a scanner so I can update the ECM on the minivan for these mods?" Arash spotted twin turbos and a reinforced chassis under the hood of Olesk's car.

Olesk dug a set of keys from his pocket and handed them to Ellie without a word. She motioned Arash to follow and they went into the barn where he and Stephanie had broken down the import tuner. Ellie unlocked a tall metal tool chest and pulled a grease-smudged laptop and an ODB2 scanner from one of the drawers. After locking everything back up again, she handed the gear over to him, warning, "Don't mess with the Wi-Fi or connectivity on this box—just use the software. It should be fully juiced." Her eyes narrowed. "You sure you're qualified?"

He chuckled and headed out of the barn. "Dare you to find me an engine I can't make purr."

"Pride's a sin." She followed behind him.

"The only sin I know—" he angled toward Stephanie and the minivan "—is a sports car with an automatic transmission."

Stephanie had the driver's-side door open and was already rolling her eyes when he arrived. He handed her the scanner and she plugged it into the information port under the steering wheel. "You going to make this one purr?" she asked with a smirk.

He opened the laptop and booted up the tuning software. She stood close to him, watching the screen. It felt like the electricity that arced from her body to his would short out all the electronics in his hands. "I'd love to," he growled quietly. Damn all of this deadly business; he just wanted her in his arms and hours and days to discover more of her strengths and mysteries.

"The engine." From the heat in her glance at him, she was thinking the same thoughts.

Knowing she was a real criminal in this gang had been the one thing barely keeping him in check. Now that he knew what she really was, and that her extensive abilities were focused on helping people, he didn't want to resist the attraction. "For now," he told her while clicking over the computer. "If you want, take a ride with me some night, to test the sync on all the systems."

"I want that." Her focus remained on the computer, where the program displayed the current settings for the minivan, but the hunger in her voice was much more primal.

How all the fuel in the car didn't ignite, he had no idea. His body burned for just a touch of her skin against his. His mind spun out, imagining the possibilities of the two of them twisted together, before coming back to the work at hand. He said through clenched teeth, "Turn on the engine."

She slid into the driver's seat and he watched every move of her body. The motor sprung to life, jarring in all of its bad timing. All of this was bad timing. Why couldn't he have met Stephanie in a garage, tuning their rides, taunting each other and racing on the midnight streets? It wouldn't matter who crossed the finish line first. They would both win.

But it wasn't simple. Of course not. A woman like Stephanie wasn't found in simple places. "Gun it," he told her. She revved the idling engine. He whispered under the noise, a vow just for her, "I will get you alone."

She whispered back, "Promise." The engine grinded louder.

The last promise he'd made was to the ghost of his friend. He looked Stephanie in the eye. "Promise."

Death was inevitable when running with people like Olesk. But now Arash had a new mission. With Stephanie. He had to fight to live.

Chapter Fourteen

Stephanie never believed promises. She believed Arash's. The vows between Frontier Justice members had been made with actions, protecting each other without question. Words usually meant little, but the way Arash told her what he wanted, there was no doubt he would find a way.

They had spent hours dialing in the modifications to the engine and updating the car's computer brain to match them. It was sometimes tedious work, with several frustrating dead ends, but Stephanie and Arash continued to operate well together. Which didn't mean things never got chippy. When they did, though, the dialogue always remained on the task at hand and never strayed to personal territory.

Wrenching on an engine had never been such a carnal experience. Their hands often met while gripping a hose or belt, and where the skin touched, the fire grew more intense. His promise kept rushing through her, stoking the flames.

Lunch had pushed them back into the social mix with the rest of the STR. The usual BS, with Thom grumbling about wanting a hand in the minivan mods. At least she could make her own sandwich and didn't have to tolerate his talk as well as frozen food.

Arash seized the opportunity to ask Olesk, "You've got us on the minivan—are we the ones driving it?"

"Yeah." Olesk came up from his food to point two fingers at Thom and Hector. "They're behind the wheels of the cargo vans."

Stephanie sorted that into the tactical data for the upcoming gig. Arash turned on Thom. "If you're not driving the minivan, you don't have to worry about how it runs."

"We started that project." Thom looked to Hector for backup, but didn't get any.

"Thank you very much, and we will finish it." Arash put the period on the conversation. Her mind turned the new information over. Her and Arash in the minivan would be good for coordinating their efforts, but they wouldn't have the same direct communication as the other vehicles and could be easily left out of the loop.

She continued to puzzle over this after lunch as she and Arash finalized the electronic component of the minivan's mods. He showed her that he was thinking on the same problem by pointing to the stock radio in the center of the console when they were huddled together in the front of the cabin. She nodded her understanding, though neither seemed to have any answers. Knowing what frequency the other cars were using would be critical ammunition for her, but snooping now was certain death.

They shut down the laptop and Ellie immediately collected it and locked it away in the barn. Trust only went so far in a gang full of criminals, and the flow of information had to be controlled. Stephanie knew that Ty and Vincent would be running all the addresses she'd given through the local and federal crime databases by now. Any open investigations on those places or people associated with them would be flagged and built on. The biggest gap in her data, the one that gaped like a bullet hole, was the date of the operation. Olesk had a habit of springing things on everyone, so it could be any minute. If she had some lead time, she could find a way to rally the rest of Frontier Justice to her.

Again, she just had to play along and collect what she could while not putting herself or Arash in any more danger than they already were. They certainly didn't give Olesk any reason to doubt their diligence. Moving from the electronics, they immediately started addressing the suspension and steering. The minivan began to tighten into a coiled snake.

Stephanie completed removing the spare tire and all its accessories, trimming weight, and walked to the whiteboard. She was about to erase the task from the list with a rag when Arash stopped her. He put his hand on her forearm and glared over at Thom and Hector. "Don't erase anything. Cross it off to show those punks how much we've done."

"If you keep needling them…" She shook her head.

"Backing down now would put me on the run."

"You don't run, do you?" Indulging him, she crossed off nearly all the tasks on the list.

"I've walked away," he said straight. "But I've never run."

"Whoever you walked from, it's their loss." She understood the difference, having done the same when she dissociated from her father's business.

"Damn right." A smile glinted in his eyes.

She placed the whiteboard in full view of Hector and Thom before joining Arash at the front of the minivan. They discussed a plan for the aftermarket shock absorbers, came up with a consensus and executed. Each step brought them closer together, either in thought or physically. She felt the significant strength of his body as he moved a part into place. Her own muscles flared, yearning for that kind of release and effort while gripping him and being held by those arms. And having those legs to wrap her own around.

Even after all the work was done for the day, her body remained charged with energy. Showering alone was such a waste when the two of them could've been naked and free to explore their bodies. But not in this house, not with Olesk and the others so close.

Arash cooked the same meal as the night before, but she wasn't bored by it. The food was real, from his hands. She was tempted to tell him about her grandmother's *hong shao rou*, but the other people in the house were coming and going through the kitchen, collecting their own dinners and taking them out to the living room. She'd made the recipe for red braised pork belly and it never took less than two hours from start to finish. She and Arash didn't have that kind of time. Maybe once this mission was over.

But that was an even bigger question. She had to stay in the moment, because each second could turn toward disaster. And each second with Arash had to be savored while neither of them knew what was coming next.

"First car you wrecked?" Arash stood and collected the plates.

She followed him to the sink and piled the pots and pans in it. The memory made her wince. "1997 Acura NSX."

"Oh, damn. The six-speed?" He clutched a fist to his chest.

"Yeah. I was seventeen years old, past midnight, driving someone else's car too fast through Half Moon Bay. Got loose in a turn, put the tail in a ditch and rolled it over." Her friends had been following in another car and hollered with more excitement than fear as she and the passenger hung upside down.

"Were you hurt?"

"Bumps and bruises." And quite a bit of shouting from her father and mother. "Hinata got a new car out of it, so no lasting damage." She leaned against the counter so her leg pressed against his. "What was your first wreck?"

"Pontiac Fiero, year unknown, owner unknown." He ran his hand through his hair and shook his head with a small smile. "I was pushing it hard, cracked the header, popped some hoses and it burst into flames. Put it sideways into a telephone pole as I was trying to get the hell out. I think the scorch mark is still on the ground."

"I've probably driven by it."

"Think of me each time you do." His leg rubbed against hers.

"You know I will." But that would be somewhere back in the Bay Area, after this mission, and she couldn't think that far ahead.

"Any more of those cookies?" His gaze lingered on her mouth.

"They were all crushed." She licked her lips.

"Wait." He pulled away from the counter and strode into the rest of the house. A moment later he reappeared at the border between the kitchen and the living rooms. Dangling in his hand were the keys to the minivan. He looked at her while speaking to Olesk and the others. "We're going to take the minivan out to test out the mods."

She approached him, each step closer making the fire in his eyes burn deeper. Over his shoulder, she saw Olesk look up briefly from his usual spot at the table with his phone. "Good idea. You'll have time to make adjustments tomorrow."

Ellie turned away from the video game Hector and Thom were playing to smile at Stephanie. "Have fun." Before Stephanie could step toward the back door with Arash, Ellie added, "There's a new development under construction a few miles to the north. Not a lot of traffic that way." She winked and turned back to the video game. Neither Thom nor Hector looked up to acknowledge anything had just happened.

"Light it up." Arash tossed her the keys. The metal was still warm from his hand.

It took all her strength to walk steadily with him out the back of the house without running her fingers through his hair and pulling his mouth to hers. The night cold didn't have a chance against the heat snapping between her and Arash. Their paths separated as they approached the unassuming minivan waiting in the dirt lot among the other cars being worked on. She got behind the wheel and he climbed in beside her.

The engine sprang to life with way more power than any minivan should. Throwing the shifter into Drive sent the car straining against the brakes. She eased off the brake and didn't even have to touch the gas to jump out to the front of the house. Hitting the accelerator hinted at the beast under the hood. Dirt sprayed behind the tires and the minivan sped onto the long drive. She twisted through the turns there, then onto the main road. The minivan tracked like it was on rails.

"Ellie said north." Arash turned in his seat to look behind them in that direction.

"We need dessert." She shot him a sly smile and turned more of the beast in the car loose, pushing them both back into their seats in a giddy rush.

"It moves." Arash nodded emphatically, face lit with pleasure.

"Like a bullet." She stepped on the gas and took them even faster down the road. And there was still plenty of power remaining. Once they reached the edge of the closest suburban development, she slowed to a more normal speed that still made the streetlights streak past.

She aimed the car at the largest glow in the development and found a strip mall with a twenty-four-hour convenience store anchoring one end. There was a pickup truck and a compact car parked out front, with a couple of bored-looking teenagers holding up one wall. The minivan fit right in, but she wondered if the hidden beast would refuse to be shut down. The engine did spin to a stop, and the whole car creaked as the bolts and welds adjusted to the transitions.

The latent energy of the ride still cranked in her. Maybe she was the beast who couldn't be controlled. Arash, too, had that wild look in his eye that only came from speed, torque and handling. They got out of the minivan and met at the front, where they stared at it. She whispered, "It looks like we're just on a milk run."

"And cookies." His carnal gaze lit onto her. The things she wanted to do with him could not be done in the light of a convenience store. She corralled her urges, for now, and headed inside. Arash angled toward the back of the store. "Bottle of water?" he asked.

"And you pick the cookies."

His growling chuckle matched the look in his eyes as he sauntered off. The danger of the operation continued all around her, and she stayed sharp to it, but she also allowed herself to feel the good in the connection with Arash. For once, she focused on her own needs. And her pulse rushed with the thrill of wanting.

She reached the front counter and asked the cashier for a package of condoms. The young white guy behind the counter was a professional and remained deadpan as he retrieved them. Arash joined them with two bottles of water and a couple different packages of cookies. He already had his cash out and paid for everything.

Outside again, Arash took the bag of goods from her and peered inside. "I thought you were prepared for everything."

She had the keys out but stayed on his side of the minivan. Each step closer to him made her breath rush faster. They met, faces close, bodies sharing heat. She reached up and ran her fingers through his hair. He leaned into the touch. She brought her mouth to his cheek and whispered the truth. "I was not prepared for you."

"I wish—" He brushed his lips against hers.

"Don't wish." She placed her palm on his chest and

curled her fingers into his jacket. "We have this, right now. I want this." A tremble started in her stomach and moved up her chest and along her arms. "I want you."

He kissed her, fierce and hungry, then pulled away. "Give me the keys." She did and they got into the minivan, him behind the wheel.

The engine blasted to life and Arash threw it into Reverse. "How's it handle?" Turning to look behind them brought him close to her again and she wanted to grab hold of his lapels and take more of those kisses until she was sated. Which felt like it would be never.

"Wound tight and ready, but you still have to ease through the transitions." The tremble continued through her. "It'll be a wreck if we push too hard too fast."

He released the steering wheel to align the edge of her hair at her cheek. "I'll drive. You navigate. We won't wreck." He backed the minivan through the parking lot. The tires chirped when he shifted to Drive, amping up her already-racing pulse. He smiled, then sped them back into the night.

Chapter Fifteen

For the first time since leaping into this nightmare of revenge and danger, Arash didn't mind that he didn't know where the road ahead was leading. In fact, he loved that pure blackness stretched out in front of him and Stephanie. Because he was with her. He finally had time to be alone with this woman who had challenged and surprised him with every turn.

His pounding heart outpaced the engine of the minivan as the modified car rocketed out of the suburbs. Stephanie had been right—it was a bullet, and if it was aimed in the wrong direction, it would kill. His focus couldn't waiver and he understood her again. Wishing for something else ignored the moment. He had to hold on to what he had. Now.

Black hills streaked past around them. Stephanie sat, alert in the passenger seat. Her gaze swept over the landscape, and when it moved across him, he felt the electric heat. She tapped her knuckle on the side window. "There's the compound."

The house was set back quite a bit from the road, but small squares of light revealed that the members of the gang were still up. Throughout the teardown and buildup of the minivan, neither he nor Stephanie had found any bugging devices, though that still didn't set his mind at ease. He held back several curses he could've used against the STR and instead stood harder on the gas. The minivan sent its own message with the throaty growl of the engine.

Stephanie smiled as they sped faster, and the thrill charged him, as well. The road north curved, giving Arash a chance to test more of the car's handling. For the most part the minivan took corners tight and blasted out of them. At the higher speed, though, a wobble shook the back end as he pushed out of a tight bank.

"Feel that?" He shifted the steering back and forth on the straightaway but couldn't reproduce it.

"Definitely." Stephanie stared into the rear of the minivan.

"We'll drop the spare back in—could use the counterweight."

"I was thinking the same thing." She tapped the side of her temple.

"That's why we're good." He put his fist out.

She bumped it. "We're better."

"And bad when we need to be." He needed to be with her.

She leaned from her seat and brought her face close to his. "Drive faster."

He stepped on the gas and the rapid acceleration pushed them back into their seats. Darkness thickened around them. The lights of the compound were long gone, and there didn't appear to be any more houses in those hills. The minivan ate up the miles and never seemed satisfied. He slowed when the road tightened into curves through a narrowing valley. Once through the pass, the land opened up flatter and the development Ellie had spoken of was dimly visible ahead.

Stephanie leaned forward to peer into the approaching collection of uncompleted houses. "We'll probably be on city streets."

He sped into the development and tested the handling in the twisting planned suburb. The shimmy was still there, but otherwise the car sprang neatly through the curves. He and Stephanie were nudged side to side, and four-point harnesses would've been much better than the stock seat belts.

The development climbed the side of a hill and he took them higher into where the more expensive houses with a view would be. Most of them were just wooden frames, but a complete house stood above all the rest. Arash took them there and parked in the deepest shadows at the edge of the development, where the last of the asphalt dissolved into the hard dirt of the mountains.

The engine spun to a stop. The car ticked and silence descended. Fabric rustled as Stephanie slid against her seat. Her hands curled into his jacket and she pulled him to her for a kiss that was heated with more power than the motor.

They parted and got out of the car, into the night. Cold air slid down the side of the hills with the aroma of mineral rock and sturdy plants. He and Stephanie huddled together as they walked toward the completed house. She carried the bag from the convenience store. Her other hand wound with his and pulled their bodies closer. "Breaking and entering?" she asked.

"It's been a while." Around the time when he was wrecking Pontiac Fieros.

"Same." He believed her ethic now, proven with all this Frontier Justice business, but he didn't fully know the person she'd been before.

Instead of approaching the front of the house, they skirted around back and across a dirt lawn with trenches cut for the sprinkler system. The rear patio spanned the entire ground floor of the house. Sliding doors at the dining area would create a huge indoor-outdoor space. Arash tested the latch. Locked.

Stephanie moved to a window just a few feet away and pried the screen off. The window opened quietly and she gestured at the wide gap. "No breaking necessary."

If there was a security system, it wasn't hooked up yet. No flashing lights or keypad anywhere. Arash slipped inside and put his hand out for her. She took the assistance, even though he knew she didn't need it, and climbed through. Any excuse for them to touch. Having her fingers laced with his in the still, quiet house shook him more than he expected. They were finally alone, in a safe place.

"Upstairs." He directed them to the stairs and they stirred the air with their ascent. The top floor explained why this was the model home for the development. A huge master bedroom overlooked the narrow valley below, with a hint of the glow from Reno in the distance.

But more inviting was the large platform bed. The two of them moved in that direction as if it had a gravity of its own. Stephanie dropped the bag next to the bed and turned to face Arash. She swept her hands up his chest, over the sides of his neck and through his hair. Each touch burned him to life. He held her waist and pulled her to him.

They kissed with no one watching, no one listening. He kissed her, knowing more of this woman than ever before. And revealing all that he was to her. She pulled his jacket over his shoulders and he tugged it off. He did the same for her and froze when he wrapped his hand around the small of her back. She was wearing a gun.

The mood frosted. Her mouth, kissing him just a second ago, was thin. "We both know how bad this can get."

"You've been carrying this whole time?"

"Since we landed in Reno." She looked him up and down. "You don't…"

"I drive better than I shoot." He always knew that however it was going to end with Olesk, it would be on the road.

"We're safe here for now." She approached him again and unzipped the front of his hoodie. "And I'm not wearing a gun if I'm naked."

SHE'D NEVER WANTED to be this naked before, and that scared her. Without a weapon or pretense or an escape route. Her need was stronger than all that. It challenged her to face Arash and her own urges.

She ran her hands across his chest and pushed the open hoodie off his shoulders. It fell to the ground, revealing the angles of his chest and waist in his T-shirt. The room was dark, but she still saw the heated glint in his eyes. He curled his hands in the hem of her sweater and tugged up. She helped him and she was soon one step closer to naked.

He sat on the edge of the bed and removed his boots and socks. She joined him there and did the same. Before she could stand again, he pulled her into his arms and joined their mouths with another kiss. Only thin cotton separated their chests and the heat built between them. His hands ranged across her back, then higher until his fingers slid through her hair. She sighed into the kiss and let herself be supported by his strength.

Her hands didn't rest, either. Each ridge of his bare arms was discovered and traced. She reached his shoulders and held on there to pull him tighter, pull the kiss deeper. He gripped her and slicked his tongue along hers. The house's central heat hadn't been turned on yet, and still she was too warm for all these clothes. She knew that her naked skin against Arash's would burn her completely, and she wanted that.

She raked her nails up his back, taking his shirt with her. He hissed a breath, then lifted his arms high so she could remove the T-shirt. His mouth returned at the side of her neck. The blaze shot white-hot through her veins.

He started to pull her T-shirt up but she leaned back to pause the motion. She carefully removed her pistol from the holster and placed it on the built-in bedside table, close within reach. Turning back to Arash, she was able to see all the contours of his muscled chest and abs in the dim light from the tall windows. With his hair down and face obscured in the shadows, he seemed mythic. But when she touched him again, she knew he was very real, warm and surging forward to her.

In a breath, her T-shirt was gone. His hands slid along her ribs, up over her shoulders, until one palm cupped her cheek. "You are so unbelievably beautiful."

"Because I'm nearly naked." A hot blush spread across her chest and up her neck.

"I thought the same thing when you were in coveralls, elbow deep in an engine compartment." Raw emotion shook in his voice.

"You didn't." Her body believed him. Heat tightened in her breasts and swirled low between her legs. But her mind couldn't yet let her be free.

"I did," he growled, hands smoothing down her arms. "And I thought you were beautiful that first night when you were powering through turns and leaving everyone in the dust." He leaned close for another kiss. It shocked her with tenderness. He'd matched her passion as they'd been clawing at each other with need. But this was different. The truth of his words was on his lips. He wanted her, she knew that, but he was willing to go slow and savor her, as well.

His kiss trailed over her cheek, then down the front of her throat. Each time he lifted his mouth from her skin, he spoke. "You. Are. Beautiful." He reached the top of her chest, leaned her onto the bed and continued to kiss down between her breasts. "Incredible. Badass. Strong. As. Hell." His mouth hovered over her belly. She trembled. Just the lightest kiss splashed shivers across her skin.

She arched up for more. He kissed the curve of her hip, then teased his teeth into the flesh. She gasped with a laugh and felt his mouth grow into a smile on her. His deft fingers undid the fly of her jeans, then popped the top button. Yes, this was what she wanted. The doubts in her brain erased.

Wiggling from side to side, she helped him remove her jeans, and she was lying on the bed beside him in nothing but her bra and panties. "Now you," she said. He stood and she missed the electricity from his close body. "Hurry."

A moment later he was back at her side. A pair of boxer briefs were the last barrier to him being as naked as she wanted to be. The electricity returned, then amplified as she touched his chest, his ribs, his hips. Each muscle responded to her, tightening as if he, too, felt the same charge.

Her touch moved between his legs and he surged forward, his arousal obvious. The need deepened in her and she shifted close enough to wind her legs together with his. One of his hands searched over her back and quickly unclasped her bra. The fabric was whisked away and his hot palm moved across one of her breasts. Her nipple tightened for more and he gave her the rough pad of his hand in light passes back and forth. Blinding heat coiled through her.

"Yes," she told him. "Touch me." Skin was freedom, and the two of them were finally pressed together, sharing all the heat, surging with their breath. She felt every ridge of his hand on her, and understood each line of the muscles of his arms and back.

Their mouths came together to wordlessly voice the hunger between them. He licked her tongue and she bit at his lower lip. Her fingers dug into his back. The lightest pinch surrounded her nipple and she moaned into his mouth.

She drew him closer with her legs, so she could grind against his erection. The room was dark, her eyes closed, and everything was so bright. Like their bodies were on the brink of turning molten. Arash separated them slightly, but their connection ran so deep now she didn't feel an absence. His hand glided across her belly, then dived down to the waistband of her panties. He waited there until she nodded, then eased slowly between her legs.

The first touch on her most sensitive skin sent a shock

wave through her. The intensity was more than she imagined and it triggered a quick fear. She gripped him and he waited again. With the roll of her hips, she showed him that she wasn't afraid. Yes, it was reckless. They ran too hot. And that's exactly what she needed.

His pace on her sex matched her. Both of their bodies surged with the movement. He kissed her mouth, her face and her neck. She stroked her fingers into his hair and held there for support as she felt herself rushing toward release. Each sensation was savored, focused on until she understood how all the nerves of her body collected Arash's touch and connected together.

"Beautiful," he rumbled. The added caress of his voice sent her over the edge. She believed him, and let herself crash into the climax. The orgasm racked her body and Arash firmed his hold around her, creating a protective cage for her to slam against.

It wasn't until she'd regained her breath that she realized she'd sunk her teeth into his collarbone. He didn't flinch when she moved her mouth and rested her head on his shoulder. The ebbing waves of the climax retained a singeing edge. She wasn't done.

Leaning up on one elbow, she drew her fingernails down Arash's chest until reaching his underwear. "Don't stop," he told her, voice like smoke. She felt his firm length over the boxer briefs, then tugged at the hem until he helped her remove them.

He filled her hand. This man, so strong and capable, was moved by her, flexing his muscles to thrust with her. The pace of his moans quickened and fired up her own needs. Her heart pounded again as she and Arash sped together through the darkness.

The rhythm stuttered and he sat up, bringing her with him. Heat focused in his eyes as he gazed at her. He leaned forward and kissed her, then gently directed her to standing in front of him. His fingers hooked into her panties and dragged them down her legs. Naked. Finally. In a house she and Arash broke into, at a bed that didn't belong to either of them. His attention moved over her and she stood, bold. A wicked smile curled his lips. She didn't see anything after that because he was kissing her belly, her hip, the top of her thigh, with his hands gripping her waist.

She stroked over his hair, wondering how her legs kept her standing. But she knew the strength came from all the need that hadn't been satisfied. Stepping away from him, she retrieved the box of condoms from the bag and pulled one out. He remained seated, took it from her and rolled it on.

Their gazes locked as she straddled him at the edge of the bed. His arms wrapped around her for support. She balanced herself with her hands on his shoulders. Face-to-face. Nowhere to hide. She lowered herself onto his length as both of them drew a long breath as one.

After a moment of discovering how they fit together, they started to rock. She rose up and he retreated. When she crashed back down, he was there, thrusting up. They moaned as one. His breath swept over her neck and her ear. He touched her in so many ways and she soaked it all in, building the fires hotter.

Too hot. That was the thrill that made her blood race so hard. Their combined strength and hunger pushed her to the verge of wrecking. Complete abandon, with the trust that they would keep each other safe. She called out again and again into the empty house. His growl shook her. She was close to delicious destruction.

"Stephanie," he whispered. Another climax sped at her. She ground deeper on Arash and he wound his arms tighter across her back. His lips stroked up her throat; his teeth brushed against her neck. She wrapped herself around him and set herself free. The release slammed through her, jolting her limbs, stealing her breath.

He held her through it all, and when she regained enough strength in her arms to scratch across his back, he lifted her up and took them both to the floor. The soft carpet cushioned her back, and Arash kept his weight off her with his arms propped on the ground. She hooked her heels around the backs of his legs to urge him on. He kissed her hard and crashed their bodies back together.

A glow burned her from within, snapping in waves to match Arash's increasing pace. "Yes, Arash." Her murmured encouragement remained close and intimate between their bodies. He grew more wild, moving their bodies with his strength. She clasped herself around him and called out his name again. He bared his teeth, thrust one more time, then locked his muscles as he came. Her own pleasure continued to swirl and the two of them stayed bound together for what felt like forever.

But it couldn't be forever. Arash shifted from her and the two of them lay on their backs on the floor, staring at the ceiling in the dim distance. He reached out and took her hand. She found her breath and whispered, "We didn't really need the bed."

"We still might." He pulled her toward him and into a kiss. How did he have so much energy? But she found that in tasting his unsatisfied hunger, her own rose again. She opened her kiss farther to let him know and his carnal grin when they separated let her know they were far from finished. "And then cookies."

Arash helped her to her feet and walked with her to the bed. The safety of the moment would only be a memory when they returned to their deadly purposes just a few miles away. Memories could be lost. This freedom wouldn't last. But the passion with Arash was real, and she would hold on to him with all her strength until the danger swept them back up again.

Chapter Sixteen

"I've stolen cars." Arash pulled the blanket tighter around his shoulders and Stephanie next to him, bringing her naked body closer to his. "Before I went straight, I stole bicycles, car parts, food." They sat on a long couch in the bedroom, facing the tall windows. The landscape was black and gray, like torn pieces of paper laid on each other. Reno glowed far away. There wasn't another person for miles around them. "Right now I'm trying to figure out how to steal a house."

"Rich people steal houses. People in power take land." She stared out the window. Emotion shimmered in her voice. "It almost happened to a friend of mine. It was the reason Frontier Justice was formed in the first place. Nineteenth-century people in the West having their lives taken, just for money. Someone had to protect them. And that fight hasn't stopped."

"I guess someone's living in the house my parents had to run from." If he could steal this house it would be for his folks. He could always find another one nearby. "They had just enough money to get out of Tehran, but they had to start from almost zero in the States."

"I'm glad they're safe." She ran her hand down his arm and held his wrist. "Glad they raised a good man."

"I wasn't always." He shifted the blanket to reach into the half-eaten package of cookies. "But my folks had been lawyers, and if I understood anything back then, it was that I couldn't be as bad as I'd been once I reached my eighteenth birthday. That's when the real consequences showed up."

"I never had consequences. We had money to take care of that." She took some cookies but just held them.

"So where'd your conscience come from?" He ate the cookie and brushed the crumbs from her bare leg.

"I got a job. My dad was furious, but I thought that if I was going to go into the family business, I had to look at all aspects." Her words floated in the dark, as if lighting more corners of her to discover. "I finally started to see that the people who took care of everything all around me were actually people. I got out of the family business and everything fell into place when a stranger who's now a friend showed up to tell me the history of my ancestor, Li Jie, and Frontier Justice."

"Sounds like a wild ride."

"It has been." She pulled closer to him and he twined his leg in with hers. "It still is."

"My friend in high school, Marcos, he didn't get out of the game when I did." None of Arash's new social circle knew about Marcos. His parents had met him back when he and his friend were teens but had dismissed him as being unreliable. Arash had never given up. "Kept trying to get him to go straight, come to trade school with me or just get a steady job at a garage. But the addiction was rough, any treatment plans were too expensive and he would just go for the fast money. He was a good driver and people were always willing to pay."

"I'm really sorry." She stroked the back of his neck in a slow, soothing rhythm.

"As soon as I had enough money, I was going to open my own garage." All of those plans were now further away than the distant dark horizon below. "There was going to be a place for Marcos there."

"What will you work on there?" She leaned her head against his shoulder. "Sport tuners? Street racers?"

"It was going to be like a neighborhood walk-in clinic. With a sliding scale for payment. People rely on cars for their work, for their lives. We would be keeping them moving."

"Like the woman with the bad piston pin in the parking lot."

"Exactly." Sadness sank into him, knowing this would probably never happen now. He might not live through the next few days. "I could make deals with parts companies to subsidize the work. And we'd have a whole training program, getting kids in there to learn."

"Training the next generation." She kissed his shoulder. "I love your idea." Her gaze rose to his and he didn't need the blanket with all the warmth in her eyes. "You have an amazing heart."

"It's just dreams."

"Some people have dreams of wielding the power to destroy and hurt people."

"I joined Olesk's gang to hurt him." How pure was his own heart?

"Because he's the one whose dreams are polluted by money and dominance. You've seen what that makes him do."

"If my ancestors had created a vigilante group, I would've joined it." Arash would never forget the stained asphalt and concrete.

"Join ours."

He stared back at her. She was serious, unwavering. He didn't doubt her heart as much as he did his own. The group she belonged to seemed so focused and organized. They reached out to help people. His only thought had been revenge. What had started as a drive to let his friend finally rest now felt selfish. But how could he shift from that when it had been his sole motor? "I'll watch your back and help how I can, but I'm not joining up with a team like yours. You're following a different set of rules."

She nodded and remained next to him. No hard sell. She wasn't just trying to make him an asset in her fight. And he couldn't think of her as that, either. Though he didn't know how to define her. He only knew that his chest felt fuller when he saw her, and his blood ran hotter when she was this close to him.

But this night with her was only a brief gasp for air before they both had to dive back under again. Where, if he wasn't careful, any second the pressure could crush him. He couldn't let that happen. Not for Marcos. Not for Stephanie, who was in as much danger, if not more.

The atmosphere on the other side of the blanket chilled and sank heavier around them. Slowly, they parted and arranged themselves. The lithe curves of her naked body disappeared under her clothes. She holstered her pistol and covered it with her jacket. He took on the armor of his jeans and boots again. It was all cold, and he could only hold on to the warmth from Stephanie deep in his core.

They collected anything personal or that could identify them, left the bed and couch in disarray and left the house through the same window they broke in. The wilds of the hills seemed closer during the walk to the car. It was late and quiet in the winter night, perfect for predators. He handed her the keys to the minivan and they climbed back into the machine.

Stephanie's face was unreadable as she started the car. The engine blasted the silence to the far corners of the valley.

"Turn it loose," he said, and braced himself on the door. She threw it in Drive, stepped on the gas and rocketed them forward. They plunged into the twisting roads of the development, and she remained incredibly calm while the tires squealed around corners and the minivan devoured the curves. The fishtailing still bothered him, but they had a solution to fix it. Though thinking about working on the car back in the space with Olesk and the STR turned his stomach.

A means to a deadly end.

"We're good." A small smile graced her face as she put the minivan through its paces.

"Yes, we are." And he didn't want to think that they were also doomed. She would survive all this. He might not, but even if he did, how could the two of them fit together in the future?

The roads straightened and the minivan shot out of the small valley. He wanted to keep the darkness all around them, like the blanket that had kept their naked bodies together and safe. The lights of Olesk's compound appeared in the hills ahead. She drove closer, the smile long gone from her face.

By the time they arrived at the house, there was only one window lit, high up in the master suite, where he supposed Olesk was with Ellie. Stephanie parked in the work area around back and they entered the house through the kitchen. Everything was quiet, the air still. After replacing the keys in the garage, he walked up the stairs with her.

They stood in the hallway between their rooms. He knew her now, and had shown her himself. They were secrets to everyone else. Reaching forward, he took her hand. She was warm and curled her strength around him. They stepped together and shared a kiss. It was brief to anyone looking, but lasted long enough for him to tell her that he would never forget her.

IT WAS A terrible night to sleep alone. Her body had rested so heavily next to him on that couch. Drifting off would've been so easy, but nothing was that simple. They'd been able to find enough safety to feed some hungers. But the need to soak in this connection with Arash and let it remind her that there was some comfort in this world couldn't be met.

The mattress on the floor in her bare room was not how she wanted to finish this night. She turned her mind to the memory of the two of them naked beneath the blanket and slowed her breath until sleep finally came.

She awoke before the dawn, startled to be so chilled and not warm in Arash's arms. Sunrise wouldn't come fast enough, no matter how much she tried to will it. Once the day started, then she could get her work done on the minivan, then maybe the gig would commence and she could wrap all this up.

As soon as the sun crested the eastern hills she was cleaned up and brewing coffee in the kitchen while arranging her breakfast. Bittersweet pain stabbed through her chest when Arash came down. This morning should be theirs. Slow. Quiet.

"Up early." His face was hard when he first arrived, but a smile creased his eyes when he looked at her.

"You, too."

He pulled out a bowl and a box of cereal. "Slept like hell." His gravelly voice tempted her back to bed all over again.

"Me, too." She poured them both coffee and they ate standing at the island.

The other members of the gang slowly came downstairs and gathered in the kitchen. Hector and Thom didn't make eye contact with either Arash or Stephanie. Like adolescents unable to process the adult world. Olesk was business as usual, but Ellie shot a sly smile at Stephanie, who returned it before hiding behind a sip of coffee.

As everyone woke up, Arash explained to Olesk about the planned fix for the minivan. There were some other logistics discussed for the other builds, and the light workday grated at her patience. She wanted to be centered on the builds and how the gig was shaping up. Too much downtime would create pockets where she would get lost in wishing for circumstances with Arash she knew could never exist.

She was the first outside, Arash quickly behind her. It took too little time to replace the spare tire in the minivan and they stood staring at the vehicle. Everything else had been dialed in and tightened down. Her hands itched to wrench on something because they really wanted to be warmed under Arash's jacket while she asked him more questions about the garage he dreamed of opening.

Hector and Thom were too protective of their builds to let either her or Arash touch them, even though she knew the work wasn't up to her standards. Olesk and Ellie were under the hood of the Subaru. There'd been no new information about the job for the Seventh Syndicate and the clock wound tight in her.

She turned to Arash. "Should we take it out again?"

"We know it'll handle great now." Sadness shadowed his face and she understood they couldn't race into the darkness again.

"There's always more—" Distant thunder rolled toward the compound. The sky this day was a clear blue. No clouds for a storm. But it was coming. The growl grew louder, metallic. She recognized the rumble of an American muscle car, tuned to intimidate.

The sound drew her and Arash away from the minivan and along the side of the house. Thom and Hector followed until the four of them stood among the parked cars in the front, watching the road. A classic Chevy approached.

Arash spoke first. "1970 Chevy Chevelle SS."

The car appeared black until it turned up the drive to the house and sunlight glinted on the angles, revealing purple iridescence. Specialized tires on custom rims moved it with sure stature. From the way it quivered going slow on the dirt drive, she saw that the car was intended for speed. Dark tinted windows hid the driver and passengers, if any.

By the time the car arrived at the front of the house, Olesk was approaching it. Ellie held back with Stephanie and the others. The Chevy stopped and the engine shut down, taking the rumble from the air around it.

The door opened and an Asian man in his twenties stepped out. Sunglasses worth at least two hundred dollars hung in the collar of his black T-shirt. Over that was a bloodred bomber jacket. His dark hair was styled in a slick wave. Olesk stepped to him and shook hands. They exchanged some quiet words while the unknown man glanced at Arash and Stephanie.

Trouble prickled up the back of her neck. The man was smooth and maintained casual confidence, but she saw the smallest twitch around his eyes when he looked at her. It was gone in a blink, but her dread remained. The man recognized her.

She tried to smooth her exterior, but Arash must've been tuned to her, or he'd seen the man's tell. Arash asked, low, "Know him?"

"No." She waited for Olesk to react as the two men continued talking, but if this new guy was outing whose daughter she was, Olesk remained perfectly neutral. "You?"

"Never seen him." Arash shook his head.

"That's David," Hector explained. "A better driver than you'll ever be."

Arash kept his gaze on David while talking back to Hector. "You've never seen me drive."

Hector spat back, "I don't need to see any of what you can do to know this guy is better."

Olesk walked David toward the others and said, "You know the old crew. But these are our latest additions, and working out very well. Wrenching, driving. Arash and Stephanie."

David stepped to Arash, hand extended. "David." He didn't speak with an accent and she was sure from his mannerisms that he was born in the States.

Arash shook his hand without hostility. "Sweet Chevy."

"Thanks, bro." David flashed a friendly grin and turned to her. "Stephanie, right?" He said it as if trying to remember what Olesk had said. She didn't buy it, but did shake his hand. He held on a fraction of a second too long.

Trip wires and traps were being set and she had to be more careful than ever. No one except her friends within Frontier Justice knew of her work there, but if David knew about her father, things could still complicate way beyond her control. Olesk had Arash steal from her father in order to prove himself, positioning her family as Olesk's rival. If he thought she was spying for Eddie Shun, she'd be dead.

"Let me show you the fleet." Olesk slapped David on the shoulder and walked them along the side of the house. The others trailed after, unmoved by the worry Stephanie felt pounding through her.

Arash, though, was right at her side. They hung back a moment and he leaned close to her ear. "Trouble?"

To keep herself and Arash alive, to keep her mission on track, she had to navigate through the next set of deadly, blind curves. "Definitely."

Chapter Seventeen

Arash had no idea who David was, but he knew that if the new man made Stephanie tighten the way she did, things would end up in a fiery wreck. And right now it felt like there was no way he could stop it.

The hoods were up on all the vehicles they'd been working on, and Olesk walked David to each. Arash and Stephanie stayed at the minivan's side while Hector and Thom discussed the cargo vans with the others. David nodded approvingly when he looked over the caged-in cargo areas. This man wouldn't be an ally. The group lingered at the engines a minute and Arash watched Thom and Hector bite back their frustration at being criticized. They had more work to do.

David swaggered over to the minivan, gaze bouncing between Stephanie and the engine. Arash held very little interest for the man and thought he could use that to his advantage. Stay under the radar until he had to strike. David braced his hands on the minivan and peered at the motor. "She's all soccer mom on the outside, but when you look under her skirt…" He barked a laugh of surprise. "Damn. What did you guys do?"

"We did our jobs," Stephanie answered flatly.

"Yeah, you did." David turned to Olesk, who was beaming. "You weren't lying. These two are assets." There was an edge in the compliment, though, something greedy that set off warnings in Arash. David checked out the cabin of the minivan, then stepped back to take in the whole. "Stealth. No one's going to see it coming. When do I get to see it move?"

Olesk spoke to the group. "Pack your kits. We're going on a test run, then moving on."

Just like that, things changed again. They were going to hit the road, where anything could happen. Arash knew that David was a fixture in this gang, and that made him a target for revenge. But the opportunity wasn't there yet. The next evolution Olesk took them through might give Arash his chance.

He and Stephanie shared a quick glance as they moved through the mudroom into the house. They walked up the stairs together and he longed for the heat they generated when this close, but the business at hand had robbed him of anything but complete focus on the potential disaster around each corner.

After packing his backpack, he reemerged into the hall to find Stephanie there, bag slung over her shoulder and expression tight. She caught his questioning look and subtly shook it off. There wasn't time or safety for analysis. He had to keep moving.

He grabbed the minivan keys from the garage and met her back at the car. The others were all assembling, a nervous energy building. With their bags stowed in the minivan, Stephanie moved toward the passenger side. "You start behind the wheel." He responded with a thumbs-up and waited by the open driver's-side door.

Olesk carefully placed a leather duffel in the Subaru and closed the trunk with a snap that drew everyone's attention. "Fifteen minutes," he said. "Thom and Hector, use that time to finalize the vans. We're taking a head start and will see who catches us first on the south side of Reno. Try not to draw too much attention, but push your machines, see what they can do for the next level." He slipped on sunglasses. Ellie got into the Subaru's passenger seat. "I'll give you the next stop once we're all clear of the city." He slipped into his car and started the engine. With precise, almost mechanical movements, he adjusted the seat, seat belt and rearview mirror, then tore up the dirt on the way to the front of the house.

Arash buttoned himself up behind the wheel of the minivan and checked his watch. Fifteen minutes would take forever. Especially because all he wanted to do was ask Stephanie what the deal was with David. But they'd never been able to be completely confident the minivan wasn't bugged and had to keep the conversation neutral.

She busied herself with plugging in the phone charger, marking the time on her watch every few seconds.

David slipped on his shades, flashed a grin and gave Arash a casual salute. "See you on the other side, soccer mom."

"Stealth." Arash saluted back. "You might not see us at all."

David disappeared around the front of the house where his Chevy was parked. Hector and Thom worked furiously on the engines of the cargo vans.

After an eternity, Stephanie announced, "Two minutes." She buckled her seat belt.

"We can't take that Chevelle." The mods on the minivan were tight, but the Chevy had been built from the ground up for speed and power.

"Not in the quarter mile, but the streets are about driving, not displacement." She brought the heat back to her gaze. "And you can outdrive him."

The reassurance helped. He had to outdrive everyone in order to stay alive.

According to his watch, time wasn't moving fast enough.

He checked the alignment of the cargo vans in the work area. "I'll let them out first, give them a surprise on the road."

"One minute." She looked over the compound, then reached back to touch her bag behind her seat.

"All set?" He put his hand on the key in the starter. Thom and Hector's engines were already turning. The Chevy rumbled at the front of the house.

"Tear it up," Stephanie said. He started the minivan and it sprang to life, ready to run. Stephanie settled in her seat. "Less than a minute." She tipped her head toward Hector and Thom. "They'll leave early."

"Punks." Arash flipped them off. Hector and Thom answered by stepping on the gas and spraying dirt as they fishtailed around the side of the house. They nearly ran into each other, then were gone.

Stephanie pulled the cuff of her jacket over her watch. "That's fifteen minutes."

Arash turned the minivan loose. It ate up the ground and was quickly in front of the house, where he had to slow to navigate through the other parked cars. David was already on the side road while Thom and Hector sped over the long drive to get there. Arash hung back so they could clear the way. Once they hit the side road, he picked up speed.

Olesk was nowhere in sight, but knowing how he liked to control the situation, he probably had trackers on all the cars. By the time Arash hit the side road, David was already entering the suburbs to the south. Thom and Hector were halfway there. Stephanie picked up her phone and tapped over it. "Once we're through the suburb there's traffic around the first on-ramp to the highway. We'll blow past to the next one a mile down."

"Affirmative." He wasn't a crook driver. She wasn't a member of a criminal gang. They worked well together and raced toward an unknown future. The road curved into the suburbs, where Thom and Hector drove more aggressively.

The vans swayed in the corners, but powered well into the straightaways. "Say goodbye." Arash stepped on the accelerator and rocketed forward. After a couple of seconds he overtook Thom, then swerved hard around him to pass Hector on the other side. Their faces gaped in the rearview mirror. And then they were gone as he sped away.

A taste of things to come. Taking them out would be easy. Olesk and David were a different story. Sweeping past the suburbs, Arash entered into the deeper traffic of the city. The first on-ramp approached, tempting with its promise of an open highway.

"There's the Chevy." Stephanie pointed to where the car was hung up in a knot of slow-moving cars next to a construction area. Arash blew past him. A second later David edged his way out of the traffic and peeled onto the city street. The morning commute had died down, leaving the lanes relatively open for a chase.

Stephanie had been right. On a straightaway, the Chevy won. He quickly caught up to the minivan and started to rumble alongside. Arash flicked him a glance, then swung hard to the right and onto a side street. The minivan handled the curve perfectly and righted itself quickly to speed off. Arash eyed the next hard turn to the left. "Putting the spare back worked."

"Feels like it." Stephanie held the handle above the window with one hand and her phone with the other. "After this left we're three blocks out from the next on-ramp." She turned to look behind them. "David's coming."

The Chevy skidded around the corner like a predator, confident in its strength. Arash powered into the hard left turn and put more distance between him and David. In another two blocks, the Chevy had caught up, but Arash had learned the strategy. "Got to stay moving." He yanked the wheel into another left, then a quick right and they were speeding up the on-ramp ahead of David.

The wide-open highway stretched south through the edge of Reno. There was more speed left in the minivan, but Arash didn't want to draw too much attention and kept it just fast enough to be able to slow to a normal pace if any cops showed up. David didn't seem as concerned with detection and brought the Chevy growling up close to the rear bumper of the minivan. He stayed there too long, then dropped back to power back into a quick pass. Arash kept his eyes ahead and didn't give David the pleasure of pissing him off.

The Chevy sped ahead but stayed in view as they neared the south edge of the city. Olesk's Subaru pulled into a nearby lane and everyone matched his speed. A couple of minutes later, the cargo vans finally lumbered up behind the group.

Stephanie's phone buzzed. "Text from Olesk." She read, "Next stop, Las Vegas." After checking her phone, she said, "About four hundred forty miles."

"I'll need to refuel along the way." Around six hours on the road, with Olesk possibly listening and a million questions Arash needed to ask Stephanie. He pointed at the radio. "You're the DJ."

She turned on the radio, found a top forty station and cranked a dance track. David flicked his headlights on and off, then surged forward and away from the others. Olesk changed lanes and edged away from Arash and Stephanie, soon disappearing among the other cars on the road. The cargo vans couldn't keep up and faded into the distance behind him.

"How much do you love Vegas?" Was that where the Seventh Syndicate gig was? He could be speeding closer to his final chance at revenge.

She adjusted her sunglasses. "It always promises more than it delivers." After typing on her phone, she held it out so he could see it, though beneath the view of anyone outside. The message read: I have a friend in Vegas.

He nodded discreetly and she erased the note. More fuel on the fire. Frontier Justice would gather around her. He would stay at her side, even though he wasn't following the same rules as her team. Once they made their play, Olesk and the others would fight to the death.

EVERY MILE BROUGHT her closer to disaster. She knew her teammate Javier was in Las Vegas, training fighters at an MMA gym, but she couldn't reach out to him on this phone. Vegas still might not be the final destination, and she had to keep her identity airtight until she and Frontier Justice went on the offensive. But despite all her work, some of her secrets seemed to be in David's hands, and he hadn't shown what his bad intentions were.

She and Arash had cleared far past Reno and skimmed along the Nevada foothills toward Las Vegas. They'd picked up drive-through for lunch and powered on, marking the distance by the loss of radio stations.

The conversation never veered from cars and motorcycles to more personal topics, though she was constantly tempted to ask him about his favorite breakfast foods and see how provocative the topic could become.

"Can you track us to the next stop?" Arash stretched his arms to the ceiling. "Time to refuel."

She swiped over her phone and located an exit. "Six miles up. Need anything from the mart?"

"Cookies." His face remained stoic.

She understood the armor he wore. "I'm into that." What if she reached over to him, took his hand or rested her palm on his thigh? The contact would contrast too hard against the real, jagged threat around them.

They arrived at the gas station in silence. Arash started fueling the car and she stretched her legs on the way into the convenience store. It was a larger one, part of a roadside oasis, filled with tourist trinkets and an expanded food section. A dozen or so travelers came and went, some looking dazed from too long on the highway.

She followed a couple women, one white and one black, into the restroom, keeping an eye on their purses. The white woman was careless and left hers unzipped, phone still awake and protruding next to her wallet. Stephanie glided past her, watching her mark and the other woman in the mirrors. Neither saw Stephanie pluck the phone from the purse and take it into the nearest stall. Closed inside, Stephanie quickly opened the phone's text app and punched in Javier's number. She messaged: Stolen phone. Hitting Vegas from Reno today. Gray minivan w/Arash. The women in the bathroom exited their stalls and went to the sink, chatting about the annoying lack of planning from their husbands. Stephanie was running out of time and typed: Olesk in blue Subaru. Two white cargo vans, custom Chevy Chevelle.

The women left the bathroom and a new wave entered. Stephanie saw that the message was sent, deleted it from the phone's log and hurried out of the stall. She caught up to the women just as the white one was checking through her purse, brow furrowed, musing, "I must've left it in the car."

"Excuse me." Stephanie approached her with the phone extended. "I think you left this on the bathroom counter."

"Oh, my God, I have to get off the road." The woman stared surprised at the phone, then gazed warmly at Stephanie. "Thank you so much." She took the offered phone and replaced it in her purse.

"You're welcome. We all do it." She smiled at the women. "Safe travels to you."

"Same to you." The white woman gave her forearm a squeeze and the black woman beamed before the two wandered off to the front door, chatting with more energy.

Stephanie shifted to the high shelves of the food mart.

She had a bag of trail mix and a box of cookies in her hands when a figure stepped into the far end of the aisle. Her shoulders flashed with a dangerous chill. David approached, a smirk on his face.

He stopped and hooked his thumbs in his pockets. "Stephanie Shun." Fired like a bullet.

But she stood facing him and didn't bleed with fear. "So you have eyes."

"I've got more than that." He swaggered a little closer. If she had to, she could drop the food and pull her pistol, but that would put an end to her entire operation. "I've got knowledge that Olesk doesn't. That's a rare commodity."

"Are you smart enough to know what to do with it?" She really wanted to slap the smug smile from his face, but she knew he was venomous and couldn't get that close until she knew his game.

"I guess you've never heard of David Huang, because if you had, you'd know I'm smart enough to drive for Olesk, earn the trust of the Seventh, and—" he licked his lips "—I want a piece of Eddie Shun's pie."

That was his angle, and she was his leverage. "The last person who tried to make a play for my family's territory was poured into a building foundation. In 1919." Not a proud moment, but she had to fight David with force.

He shrugged. "Times have changed. And Eddie Shun's daughter is driving for the STR, even though Olesk doesn't know who she really is." His smile faded. "And if you want to keep it that way, you're going to give me the routes and runners for your father's insurance business."

What David and her father referred to as *insurance* was just old-fashioned extortion. One of the uglier sides of her father's business, but he hadn't needed to resort to intimidation for years and sometimes found a way to put the money back into the neighborhoods. In the hands of David, though, she was sure it would be a reign of terror.

She tried to plan a pivot out of his trap but couldn't create a move that wouldn't throw her completely off balance. "I'll have to think about your generous offer."

He laughed. "You have until Vegas." Turning on his heels, he glided out of the aisle and out of the market.

A handful of hours. Handing David the names of her father's runners and their routes would definitely lead to bloodshed in San Francisco. But what would happen if David told Olesk who she really was? Disaster. Even if she managed to battle her way away from Olesk and the STR, it would mean that all the work she'd done to take down the Seventh Syndicate and their human trafficking would be for nothing. She knew the big operation was close and had to be there.

In the middle of this web was Arash. Her heart ached knowing that he thought he'd heard all her secrets. He trusted her, and she was about to prove that he shouldn't. The only strategy out of the traps David had just set would lose her Arash forever.

Chapter Eighteen

People came to Vegas for the party, the gambling, the spectacle and the opportunity to pretend there were no consequences, but all Arash could see was the traffic. They'd hit town near sundown and abandoned the speed and freedom of the highway. Cars crawled all around them, wandering, cruising, not knowing where they were going. Rideshares and taxis prowled for gaps between cars and darted into them for any advantage.

Tightening Arash further was the stormy silence that had taken Stephanie since they'd stopped for gas. They were still trapped in the minivan, leaving no opportunity for open discussion. He'd motioned his concern for her and she'd gestured as if everything was fine. She'd even written another note on her phone, telling him not to worry, she was sorting strategies.

But it had seemed worse than that. And he had a feeling it had something to do with David, who he'd spotted on the highway a few minutes after leaving the gas station. What the hell was the deal? David could be an ex. Or he might know about Frontier Justice. The man was playing it so cool and confident, it was obviously the long game.

Arash tore himself up inside with the questions as they inched toward the hotel Olesk had texted Stephanie shortly after they'd arrived in the city. She swiveled her head around, keeping an eye on all the cars around them.

At one point she tapped his shoulder and indicated something behind them. The two cargo vans were a couple hundred yards behind.

He nodded to her. "What do you say we get a fancy dinner?" Thousands of dollars of cash hung heavy in his jacket and backpack.

"Shower first." But she didn't sound too enthusiastic.

"These nice hotels have spas, right?" He'd walked through them but never stayed. "I'm gonna get myself buried in hot stones." A possible preview of a shallow desert grave, if everything went to hell the way it felt like it was.

"I could see you in a seaweed wrap." Her smile was too brief.

"How about mud wrestling? That's a thing, right?" He was trying too hard and it tightened cold coils around his heart.

"Mud *bath*," she explained with a small smirk. It was all they could manage and fell back into silence. They finally reached the hotel and Arash took them into the self park. The minivan sighed relief when it was turned off and ticked as it cooled. Arash was already cold. Desert winter stole any moisture from his body. He clenched a fist to convince himself he still had the strength to fight. They collected their bags and locked the car up. It looked as ordinary as everything else around it.

Arash, though, felt like everyone would be able to see the dark tension radiating out of him. He and Stephanie were halfway to the elevators when Stephanie broke the silence. "I'm going to tell you something before the others find out, and you have to know that this—"

"How's the soccer mom?" Olesk approached from another aisle of the parking lot, Ellie at his side. Neither had their bags, so they must've reached town a little while ago.

Arash clamped down on his worry about what Stephanie was about to tell him. She transitioned amazingly to a neutral face and answered, "She's a killer in disguise."

It was so damn close to the truth. Neither Arash nor Stephanie were what Olesk believed. Arash wanted to draw his knife and end it all right here in the parking lot, just so he could learn what Stephanie's next secret was.

Olesk laughed. "I like that. She's going to kick ass in LA."

Arash coiled tighter. It wasn't going to end in Vegas. He unclenched his jaw to ask, "We going to have time for dinner?"

"We're overnighting." Olesk slid his glance to Ellie.

"I already made reservations." She grinned back.

"But first…" Olesk paused as they reached the elevators. "We're meeting up in our suite, 1265." Arash felt the slightest shimmer of tension from Stephanie at his side. The others didn't react and couldn't have detected it. Olesk continued, "Arash, go check in. It's under my name, with your first name. We'll meet you up there."

"And my room?" Stephanie kept a casual posture, hand on the strap of her bag, but Arash knew it was a lie.

Ellie smiled slyly. "For the sake of economy, we put you two in the same room. Hope you don't mind."

"Not at all." Stephanie turned to Arash and he saw the storm continuing behind her eyes. "You?"

"I know how to pinch a penny." Nothing was real anymore. Everything he saw or heard was hiding another layer of doom.

Olesk chuckled and swung the side of his fist into Arash's shoulder. It took all of Arash's composure not to twist Olesk's arm up with his and yank his shoulder out of its socket. Ellie punched the elevator button and Olesk said to Arash, "We'll see you up there." His look shifted to a walkway opening nearby, with a sign pointing to the lobby above it.

Arash locked his gaze onto Stephanie's. "I'll be there." She nodded back in what looked like an attempt to reassure him. He knew she had her pistol. And skills beyond that. But maybe she wasn't the one who would be in danger up in that suite. He could be the one in the crosshairs.

The elevator dinged and opened for Olesk, Ellie and Stephanie. Arash held on to Stephanie's look as long as he could, until the doors closed. After a steadying breath, he hefted his bag higher on his shoulder and headed into the casino.

Lurid video screens flashed and a thousand bands played a thousand songs from the speakers, all cheerful and lively. More lies. He knew that it was all created to draw blood.

Most of the people in the casino were focused on the games, drifting in awe of their surroundings or working. One figure lurked at the periphery of Arash's vision. He knew it was David. As he passed an interior elevator bank next to a busy bar, his suspicion was confirmed. David flashed his room key card to a security guard and glanced quickly back at Arash before disappearing among the people at the elevators. The arrogant smile on David's face meant all kinds of trouble, and Arash seemed to be the last person to know what was about to come crashing down.

He stood impatiently in line at the front desk. Every delay ahead of him shaved his patience to a sharper edge. By the time he got to the black man at the computer he thought he'd just bark out his needs. Arash, though, managed to be civil and the desk agent was efficient and quick with the transaction.

Arash thanked him, stuffed the keys in his pocket and hurried toward the elevators. Of course some drunk jerk thought it was the perfect time to cut him off and angle the two of them into a set of unused slot machines. Arash warned, "Careful, man," and put his hand on the shorter Latino man's shoulder, feeling nothing but solid muscle.

The man with slick hair and tattoos on his hands peered into Arash's face and didn't look drunk at all. "You're a good guy?"

"No." From the scars on his knuckles and the bump on the bridge of his nose, Arash knew this man was a fighter, but he would take him on if he was going to stand between him and the elevator to Stephanie.

"Me, neither." The man grinned crooked. "But I'm not a bad guy either, Arash." Hearing his name coming from a stranger set off all kinds of alarms. Arash took a step back, scanned the area for anyone else coming and balanced for combat. The man put his palms out as a peace offering. "Friend of Stephanie's." But which of her identities? Arash kept his guard up. The man edged closer and lowered his voice. "Frontier Justice."

Arash shifted his perspective on the man and lowered his defenses. A little. "How'd you find us?"

"She messaged me the cars you all were driving and I put the word out to my Teamster and cabbie friends." The man's awareness kept scanning the people around them. Arash did the same, but didn't recognize any of Olesk's people. "We've got cops and Feds on our side. They found your picture." He extended a thick hand. "I'm Javier."

"Glad to meet you." For once, Arash was telling the truth. He shook his hand. "Who the hell is David?"

Javier shrugged. "No idea. You tell me."

"Part of Olesk's gang. Asian American guy. He showed up yesterday and got Stephanie super nervous."

"I'll let the others know." Javier pulled out his phone. "What else you got?"

"I've got to hurry and meet everyone in Olesk's suite, 1265." Any unusual delays would definitely be noted by Olesk. "Stephanie and I are in 810."

"Same room?" Javier cocked his head.

"You her mother?" Arash wasn't in the mood to explain everything to this guy he just met.

Javier swelled slightly, something that would intimidate most people. "I'm her friend."

"Then trust her to make her own decisions." Arash was running out of time and shifted gears. "We're going from here to LA. Cargo vans are kitted to fit about sixteen people each. Olesk rolls with a 9mm, don't know if the others are armed."

"Good stuff, man." Javier stepped out of the way, clearing the path to the elevators. "Stay safe. Tell Stephanie I said the same to her. Or don't, depending on who's listening."

"You know it." Arash nodded him a salute. "Thanks."

"Thank me with beers and a brawl sometime."

"Count on it." Arash stepped away from Javier and into the flow of people in the casino. He didn't bother looking back. Javier would be gone by then, but watching. Arash had expected the vigilante group to be filled with starched, serious types, not a regular guy like Javier. Stephanie wasn't straitlaced herself, though. If he really did know her. Arash just hoped that her group was up to taking on Olesk and the Seventh.

The elevator ride up was filled with a giddy tourist family speaking what he thought was Hindi. A little boy kept staring at Arash. The smile Arash returned sent the boy behind his mother's leg for safety. Smart kid.

Arash got out on the twelfth floor, found Olesk's suite and knocked. A second later, Ellie answered and welcomed him in. All of the STR hung out on the dark chairs and couches of the wide living area. It was a shame the curtains were drawn, Arash knew the tall windows would've given an incredible view. Stephanie sat by herself on one side of the room. Her face was neutral, but her darkness still shimmered. David was the only one who seemed upbeat. Hector and Thom slouched, tired in their seats, nursing sweating bottles of beer. The same kind that Ellie drank as she perched on the edge of the couch where David was.

Olesk offered Arash a bottle from a twelve pack in a cardboard box, but he waved it off. "Maybe after a shower."

"I won't keep you guys long." Olesk stepped to a low coffee table in the middle of the living area and set the bottle down near one corner. "This is the pickup. 8:00 a.m., so if you hit the road after 3:45 a.m., you're already late." Everyone leaned forward in their chairs and Arash stepped closer. "Cargo vans get filled with cargo." Arash's stomach roiled with acid. Cargo was a terrible way of describing a person. "Me and David are rolling close supervision. Soccer mom one level farther out keeping watch." Arash glanced to Stephanie and she nodded. Olesk retrieved another bottle of beer and placed it on the corner diagonal from the first. "This is the drop-off. Airfield. 11:00 a.m. wheels up, no waiting. Once the cargo is off-loaded, we scatter."

But no addresses, so if he or Stephanie could contact Javier again, there were scant details to deliver.

Olesk picked up the first beer and twisted off the cap. "I've been monitoring all channels, and I haven't found a whisper of resistance, so the biggest thing we need to worry about is accidental contact. Be smooth. All good?"

Hector put his fist out for Thom and the other man bumped it before Hector answered, "Sounds like a plan."

"Got it." Arash amped up, edgy. The whole STR team would be at the pickup point. That was his chance to pick them apart. "Dinner?" He delivered it only to Stephanie. If he could get her alone, then she could tell him what the hell was going on.

Stephanie stood, but instead of stepping to Arash, she turned toward David. "First, David has something he wants to tell you all."

David rose to his feet, schooling his surprise to a smug turndown of his mouth. "Are you sure?"

Stephanie dripped disdain for David as she shifted her attention away from him and to Olesk and the others. Adrenaline pumped hard up Arash's legs and down his arms as he prepared to fight his way out of the room.

Stephanie said calmly, "Since David doesn't have the guts to tell you, I'll come out and admit that I'm Eddie Shun's daughter."

Dead silence. Except for the scream of Arash's pulse in his ears. He tried to make the new information fit with the other razor-sharp puzzle pieces he'd been forcing together. He'd stolen from Eddie Shun in order to get into the gang. She must've known that. But she still helped him.

And now Olesk was staring at her like she was a cobra spitting venom in the hotel room. Ellie watched Olesk, as if waiting for direction. Hector and Thom gaped and David shifted his gaze between Stephanie and Olesk.

Stephanie continued with unnatural stillness. "David was waiting for just the right moment to tell you. Or maybe he wasn't going to, depending on whether or not I gave him some intel so he could chisel into my father's business."

David surged toward her but held himself back. Arash instinctually angled to put himself between the possible attack and Stephanie. But who was he protecting? Who the hell was Stephanie?

"He was playing angles outside the STR." Stephanie lit her killing gaze back onto David.

David jutted his jaw and pointed at her with his fist. "What we really need to be asking is what is Eddie Shun's daughter doing in the STR? Right, Olesk? What is she doing here?"

Olesk faced her, hands open and ready. His flannel shirt was buttoned but untucked and could be hiding his automatic. "Okay. What *are* you doing here?"

Stephanie's body language remained unaggressive. He remembered how close they'd been when he discovered she was armed. He'd thought then that he knew her. She spoke now without apology. "I'm driving. I'm fixing up these cars for this gig. I'm making my own name." She glared at David. "Because I hate it when people only think of me as Eddie Shun's daughter."

It was very convincing. As convincing as when she'd told Arash that she'd gotten away from the family business but didn't say exactly what it was.

"You stole from Eddie Shun's warehouse." Olesk shifted to include Arash. "Did she say anything when she was driving you out of there?"

"Nothing about it at all," Arash admitted. The getaway replayed in his mind with this new lens. He'd originally attributed her concern about shooting at their pursuers to an unusual ethic. It had been one of the things that had first made him regard her as anything other than a criminal. But she could've just been trying to not get the security men hurt because they were her father's employees.

"She didn't tell you who her father was at *any* point?" Ellie narrowed her eyes and cocked her head at Arash.

Arash answered with his gaze on Stephanie. "No." Stephanie blinked, pain in her eyes for a second. Then she was hard again.

Ellie muttered, "Super awkward."

David's voice rose. "Who gives a damn what she tells her boyfriend? I'm not comfortable with her in the STR."

Stephanie shot back, "You would've been plenty comfortable if I'd given you the information you wanted."

David fumed and looked more desperate as he went to Olesk. "You can't believe anything she tells you. You and I have rolled together through some serious business." David showed his teeth. "Life and death, remember?"

All of Arash's chaos cleared for a moment. He knew whose death David was talking about.

Olesk's face calmed to a stone mask and he asked David, "Did you try to leverage her?"

"No." David blinked too many times. "I was waiting until we were all here to say something, so she couldn't worm out of it."

Stephanie scoffed, "You were waiting so long I had to say it for you." A more dangerous emotion darkened her voice. "I could be at dinner right now."

David's face reddened. "Where you'd be figuring out how to twist things—"

"I got it." Olesk hovered his hands over his ears as if ready to cover them against the argument. "I got it. Both of you shut the hell up. Shut the hell up and drive. That's what you're paid to do. Can you do that?"

"Absolutely." Stephanie's expression frosted.

Olesk stared at David while David looked incredulous. After a second he blurted, "Of course," as if he didn't have to say it at all.

"Anything else?" Stephanie shifted her balance toward the door.

"You tell me." Olesk scanned everyone in the room. "Anyone else have a bomb they want to drop?"

Arash did. But it would have to wait until Olesk was lined up in his sights. If he could make it to Los Angeles without being blindsided again by Stephanie.

Thom broke the silence. "Henry Ford is my father." He chuckled and drank from his beer.

Hector clinked his bottle against Thom's. "Carlos Chevy is my father."

Olesk pointed at the door. "Everybody get out of my suite."

Hector and Thom were the first to go, murmuring to

each other and suppressing laughs. Stephanie told Olesk, "We'll be on the road by 3:30 a.m."

"Good. Less talking, more driving." He spoke to Stephanie, Arash and David as if he was addressing children. "We have a big gig tomorrow for big people. We make them happy, we get happy, too. We make them sad, we get dismembered."

"Understood." Arash saluted Olesk and headed for the door. Stephanie caught up with him and they stepped into the hallway together. He pulled one of the room keys from his pocket and handed it to her, careful not to touch her skin and test whether or not the heat remained. "810."

She murmured, "I know there was a better way for you to find out..."

He stopped in the hall to face her. "Damn right—" David stood outside Olesk's suite, glaring at them from over a dozen yards away. Arash resumed walking to the elevators. Stephanie stayed with him, both silent until the doors closed.

She started quickly, "I understand that this is a complete wreck, but I wasn't lying to you."

"About what, about which identity?" He stared at her, this woman he'd been completely naked and exposed with, and didn't know who she was. "Javier's downstairs somewhere, and I bet your father's people are out here, too, ready to put a bullet in me if they found out I was with you."

"He doesn't do that kind of thing." She stood up to him, jaw set.

"Not if his only daughter was caught running around with a car thief?"

"That's not what you are."

No, he hadn't been that for a very long time. And he'd only returned to that world for revenge. But then he met Stephanie. "Who knows who anyone is?"

The elevator stopped two floors down and more people

got on. He and Stephanie turned from each other and he swallowed so many words, rage and confusion that they choked his heart. At the ground floor he moved off quickly. It didn't take long before he spotted Javier pretending to play a slot machine. Stephanie saw him, as well. She turned to Arash, pain shimmering in her eyes. He hated seeing it. He hated feeling the same in himself. And he had no idea how to end it. He tipped his head toward Javier, telling her to go. Then he walked away in the opposite direction.

Chapter Nineteen

The screen on the video slot machine tried desperately to capture her attention. Panthers prowled through a jungle scene, tigers snarled and claw marks slashed out to mark the matches in the indecipherable grid that fell into place each time she pushed the button. But she moved automatically and her divided mind had no space for the game.

Javier sat next to her, both of them angled away from each other so it didn't look like they were together. She spoke just loud enough to be heard over the din of the machines, but kept her words contained to just the two of them. "3:30 a.m. departure. We have to be somewhere in LA by 8:00 a.m. for the pickup. We're delivering—"

A cocktail waitress came by and Stephanie declined. Javier stopped her. "Beer, and a lot of luck."

"I'll see if we have any left." The white woman with an Eastern European accent flashed an easy smile.

She continued her rounds and Stephanie resumed her debrief, focusing on the details in order to keep her emotions from spiraling her into darkness. "Delivering to an airfield. Wheels up at 11:00 a.m., so have Vincent check registered flight plans for every small airport in the county."

Javier murmured back, "I got that, but I'm sure he knows his job, being a Fed and all."

She ignored his correction. "No indication if the Seventh will be there."

"They're not going to leave a job this big unsupervised," Javier exclaimed with disappointment and tried to show people how close he was to a jackpot on the screen, but no one paid attention. When he brought his attention back to the machine, he sassed, "I met your man."

She choked out, "He's not my man."

"He was all puffed up and postured like he was a few minutes ago."

"Things changed." She'd known that telling the crew the truth about her father could get David off her back. It was a stick of dynamite, and the blast wrecked the best thing she had with Arash.

The cocktail waitress returned with Javier's beer and he overtipped her. The woman thanked him and added, "They're brewing up a fresh batch of luck right now, so it shouldn't be long."

"I'm good, thanks." He toasted her with the beer. "But bring some to this woman here." He hooked his thumb at Stephanie. "I think she could use it."

"Coming right up." The cocktail waitress smiled her way off.

Javier darkened in her peripheral vision. He barely said, "Things always change." She didn't know the man that well but had heard from his closer friend Ty that he'd gone through a rough breakup within the last few months.

It would've meant the world to get a beer of her own and allow the two of them to pour out their feelings, but the mission was far from over. Her throat was so tight she could only manage to say, "I hadn't told him who my father was."

"And he found out?" Javier stood to put more cash in the machine.

"When I told the rest of the gang. I had to get out from under some leverage David Huang was putting on me." Saved her skin. Paid a huge price.

"Damn…" Javier put his empty beer down and kept

playing. "And Arash gets KO'd." He punched the button on the machine and spun on his stool before returning to the screen.

"Totaled." She hit the cash-out button and stood to leave. Time was up; she knew to avoid suspicion from any STR members who might see her, she couldn't sit next to Javier too long. And if she kept talking about how she'd just shattered Arash's trust, she wouldn't be able to keep herself composed.

Her machine spit out her ticket and Javier handed it to her. "You won."

"I lost." She gave the ticket back to him and disappeared into the noise of the casino.

Frontier Justice knew everything she did. All the intel collected over the course of these grinding, tense days drained out of her. The job wasn't done yet, though. She had to keep her energy up for at least another sixteen hours. Los Angeles would determine if this mission was a success.

Everything else rang hollow with failure. She drifted through the casino and into an expansive multilayer indoor mall. Artfully crafted displays highlighted expensive purses and clothing. No color was bright enough, no metal shiny enough or matte smooth enough to catch her eye.

The trust between her and Arash had fused under such harsh conditions that it was stronger than she'd known with anyone else. Like he knew her. But he hadn't, and when he learned, their connection snapped like a bone.

Arash had been focused on his revenge throughout their time in the STR and she didn't see him wavering now. The mission for both of them would likely move forward. What it meant for the two of them, though, she couldn't predict.

The last person on earth she wanted to see came striding up the walkway. David wore a fake smile and fury in his eyes. She stood and waited for him to reach her, knowing that there were far too many security guards and cameras for him to try anything physical.

He attacked with a hiss, "You think you're so smart."

All emotion drained from her face. "This was all your idea. And now you've learned what the few people stupid enough to try have learned." She sharpened her voice. "No one corners me."

"But it doesn't end that easy." His fists remained at his sides. "Not after you messed with me in front of Olesk."

"You lit the fuse, David." She wanted to condemn him for what had happened with Arash, but she knew it was her own fault for not telling Arash about that detail of her history sooner. "Don't blame me for getting burned."

David sneered a laugh. "We'll see who's still intact after all this." He leaned close. "If it's just you and me without your boyfriend…" Trepidation shimmered in his eyes when he looked over her shoulder. He tried to maintain his swagger as he took a step backward. "Watch your rearview," he warned, but it didn't have much impact as he was retreating.

After David strutted off into the mall and slipped around a corner, she turned to look where he'd been staring. A flush of heat wrapped around her ribs when she saw Arash standing a few dozen yards away. His hair was down, surrounding a still, dark face. No wonder David turned tail. The menace emanating from Arash could move mountains. The glow in her chest twisted to an ache. He'd been looking out for her, but now that David was gone, Arash turned and joined the masses of people at the edge of the casino. As he disappeared, all the warmth in her body left with him.

THE MOST EXPENSIVE meal of his life and Arash didn't taste a bite. He sat at the crowded bar of an Asian–South American fusion restaurant in the hotel while small plates appeared before him. The artfully prepared high-concept food might've been delicious. High television screens showed sporting events, but his attention was on the mirror behind the bar, where he could scan the room and a little bit into the casino.

Stephanie was in the restaurant, at a table with her back to the wall. He couldn't remember if he'd followed her or if she'd appeared after he'd taken his seat. None of the other STR members showed up. He'd kept a specific look out for David, but that man had been a no-show after the brief incident in the mall. The snake had sent this whole situation into a skid. Arash still didn't know what to think about Stephanie's latest secret, but he did know that he was a day away from finally getting Olesk and he couldn't miss this chance.

Arash watched her in the mirror. He didn't want to. He wanted to be seated across from her at the table, experiencing the food with her. Or they could order room service and spend the night discovering. There was no freedom for that now. Time was in short supply, and he didn't know how long it would take for him to trust her again. If ever.

He continued to eat, but nothing filled the cold, hollow space in his chest. All the bottles of booze glowing on their lit shelves tempted him with a night of numbness. 3:00 a.m. would come fast, though, and he had to be ready.

It took only a split second of him looking down at the dish of fried plantains and tempura shrimp being delivered to discover that Stephanie had disappeared from her table. She was standing next to him, by the empty seat at the bar. "May I?" The place was busy all around her, and she was so very still.

"Sure." But what could she say that would change any of this?

"I'm sorry." She sat next to him. The bartender came by, and she ordered a cocktail and waited for him to leave. She looked at Arash in the mirror. "I should've told you. I didn't want it to be important. I wanted it to just be you and me."

"And Frontier Justice." He kept his voice down.

"No." She turned to him. "Not when we were alone in the dark. That was me."

"Not all of you." He stared forward, seeing her straighten her posture in the reflection.

"You don't know." Emotion shook her voice. "You don't know how much of me you saw. I showed you more than anyone…" She steadied herself and faced the mirror again. "My father isn't who I am. He doesn't know about Frontier Justice. He trusts me because he knows that my decisions are my own." The bartender slid her drink in front of her. She pulled out too much cash for it and laid it on the bar. She edged closer to Arash, sparks of heat arcing between them, and he couldn't tell if they fed the emptiness inside him or highlighted how deep it was. "I should've told you. Now you know."

The drink remained untouched. She stepped from the bar and left the restaurant.

Arash pushed the plates away from him and settled his bill with cash. It didn't seem like he'd ever be hungry again. He picked up his backpack and threaded his way from the restaurant and into the casino. Halfway to the elevators he spotted Javier at a bank of video slot machines. The man glanced pointedly at the empty space next to him, then resumed playing. Arash went there and slipped cash into the machine, expecting more tactical information from the shady vigilante group.

Javier asked casually, "What's the name of the first teacher you had a crush on?"

It took some effort to keep from turning to Javier. Instead, Arash growled back, "I'm not telling you that."

"So you have secrets, too, like Stephanie." Javier didn't take his gaze from the machine in front of him. "Some things aren't easy to bring up, right? I mean, I could tell you all about Mrs. Dominguez and the way she looked when she sat on the edge of her desk, but you don't want to tell me your stories."

"I get it." Great, now he was getting schooled by a guy he barely knew. Even if Javier was right.

"Then don't screw it up." Javier revealed the skull tattooed on the back of his right hand when he slipped another bill into the machine. "Remember who the bad guys are."

"I know who they are." Their grinning, heartless faces had been burned into his mind as soon as he'd met them. "I didn't know who she was."

"Do you now? Learning who her father is explains her?" Javier drank from a bottle of water and snuck a glance at him.

The question rang in Arash's head. "No." Discovering her had been the thrill. She was more than he'd ever know.

"Watch her back." Javier cashed out. "Vincent the Fed will be in LA by the time you get there. Kick ass tomorrow." He wove into the crowd.

Arash left his machine with money remaining. Maybe it would bring someone else luck. Better than him holding on to the cash from Olesk's jobs. He made his way to the elevators, then the eighth floor.

Stephanie was already in the room. The lights were off and the curtains were open to show the glittering landscape below. She sat on the edge of the large bed facing him, with her coat and boots off, but otherwise dressed. Flashing video displays outside glinted off her pistol on the nightstand.

Arash closed and locked the door, then double-checked the lock. He walked deeper into the room, feeling her gaze on him, and dropped his backpack by the long couch before looking about the room. "Are we alone?"

"We are." She shifted, curling one leg onto the bed to angle toward him.

"Did David make another play?" Arash took off his

jacket and laid it over the arm of the couch. He sat to take his boots off and stretched out his feet once they were free.

"No sign of him. He probably won't try something until tomorrow's gig is over." Half of her face was in shadow, half was painted with the dim colors from outside. "Did you have any trouble?"

"Just Javier telling me to tell you Vincent will be in LA by the time we get there. Then he schooled me."

"About Frontier Justice?"

"About you." The room settled quiet.

She adjusted her posture, defensive, and straightened the sides of her hair. "What did he say?"

"He said all the right things, which is better than you and I had been doing." A thousand miles separated them. He was a heartbeat away from reaching for her.

Stephanie moved again, brought both legs up onto the bed and leaned back into a stack of pillows. The rustle of the blankets and crisp cotton should've been surrounding him, instead of being that far in the distance. He turned on the couch and extended himself along the length. Checking the watch that she had bought him, he saw that if he fell asleep in the next nine minutes, he'd have five hours of rest until the alarm rang.

He asked, "Did your father want you to get into the family business?"

"He wouldn't have fought it if I'd gone into the management side." She settled deeper into her nest. "But he was furious when I was running with his street-level crew."

"That's where the real action is."

"And the real trouble," she said. "I learned the stakes, the consequences of what we were doing. I learned that I'd be better at helping people than taking from them."

"The last car I stole for a joyride had a faulty starter and the driver's-side window didn't roll down. I took it two blocks, parked it and walked away when all I wanted to do was fix it." He'd fixed a lot of cars since then. He couldn't help fix Marcos's life before it was cut short.

"You're going to make that shop happen."

"Sometime after tomorrow." Neither of them knew what would happen in the next twelve hours.

His own garage had been a secret fantasy. If he lived past the next day, it might still be a possibility. But it seemed as if the metal and concrete would be that much colder if Stephanie wasn't there, sleeves of her coveralls rolled up, bringing a broken engine to life.

Stephanie worked her phone. The glow shined in her eyes. "3:00 a.m. alarm."

He got up from the couch and pulled the folded blanket that lay across the foot of the bed. She curled the remaining blanket up from where he should've been lying next to her and brought it across her clothed body. He got back on the couch and dragged his blanket over him. "Can't wait." Revenge. Finally. But what would that leave him with afterward?

"Good night." Her phone went dark, and so did her face.

He hated how the air cooled and stilled between them. His mind had processed all the new information about her, but the shocked burn of betrayal still lingered in places he couldn't find to extinguish. They were deep and had remained unknown until he'd met Stephanie. "I've got your back."

"Thank you." Her voice glided through the quiet room like slow lightning. "I'm with you."

"Good night." He wrapped her words around him. They were warm from her breath and body, and slowed his heart until he could close his eyes and sink into the couch.

They both woke before the alarm. He heard her shifting in the bed and opened his eyes to the same level of darkness as when he'd fallen asleep. The sun wasn't close to rising, but he stretched his body to standing and flexed his muscles to pump blood into them. Stephanie holstered her pistol and pulled on her jacket. He washed up in the bathroom, then traded places with her. By the time she was returning to the bed, he had his boots and jacket on, his backpack over his shoulder. She laced up her boots, grabbed her bag and picked up her phone to cancel the alarm.

"Los Angeles?" His pulse kicked into a higher gear.

"You drive," she said. "I'll navigate. We won't wreck."

On the other side of the door they were criminals, secret vigilantes and seekers of vengeance. There were no guarantees once they crossed that threshold. He stepped to her and she moved closer. Her face tipped to his and he leaned down. They kissed. A simple, small gesture that concentrated all the heat in his chest. She balled her fist in his jacket and he gripped her shoulders.

The kiss parted, they separated and walked through the door.

Chapter Twenty

They were on the road for three hours before the sun came up. Drive-through breakfast had been bought and eaten. The minivan had been refueled. Stephanie had searched through radio stations and waited for word from Olesk. Arash drove with stern focus and appeared calm, but she knew the storm raging inside.

Today.

The sun rose and marked the beginning of the day they'd both been working toward. Tension churned deep in her, growing with each mile closer to Los Angeles. The bright morning had no clouds. Shadows stretched from the semis and smaller cars across the highway. She hadn't spotted any other STR members. There'd been no communication. Olesk was expecting loyalty and precision from his team. She prepared herself to ruin his plans.

With only scant details, she couldn't fully predict how the operation would play out. But she carried one certainty with her. Nothing Olesk or the Seventh Syndicate could throw at her would change the steady, reassuring heat from her kiss with Arash this morning. They'd traversed rough territory to get there, but it only proved that what they were together was worth fighting for.

So many lives at stake. The safest choice would be to run away. She would never. Arash sped them southwest, to the lost people who needed her help. To the people who needed justice.

Less than an hour away from Los Angeles, a text came through. "Olesk." She read, "San Pedro." Then an address she punched into her mapping app.

Arash shook his head. "I don't know where San Pedro is."

"Near the port. Near Long Beach. On the far end of the city." Which explained why he'd given them so much time to get there. "The airfield might not be far from that, but in LA, distance is set in time, not miles. Two blocks can take half an hour."

Arash pushed the minivan faster, then had to slow as they moved into the traffic of more populated areas. She checked the time and the map; they would be on time. The highway turned into a freeway. Traffic choked the lanes. Aggressive cars bolted into the smallest gaps as they jockeyed for advantage.

She watched the frustration grow in Arash. His posture straightened, and his fists gripped the steering wheel. "With what this minivan can do, we could tear this up. We'd blow away anyone else out here." But they remained stealthy and moved with the normal flow.

After typing a note on her phone, she tapped him on the arm and held it up to him. *Soon.*

Arash nodded, face stony. Eyes blazing like a predator.

A cold wind swept across the city to howl a chorus against the body of the minivan. Black road grime swirled at the edges of the freeway, where the lost ladders, torn-off bumpers and shattered tires collected.

She slowed her breath and spun the ring around her finger. Pistol, knife, phone fully charged. She knew who the major players were in the operation, what they were driving and the address of the first destination. After waking before dawn, crossing a desert and a state line, and piercing through a city's traffic, they were two miles away.

The navigation took them off the freeway and down onto the streets of a partially industrial neighborhood. Warehouses and processing plants passed the windows, then rows of old, single-story houses and an ancient grocery store with a faded sign.

"Two blocks." Her awareness cranked high, marking every car around them and checking for anything that might seem irregular in the area. "Then left. It'll be on the right."

Arash cruised deeper into the neighborhood and slowed at the address. It was an old, abandoned movie theater. Her heart caught in her throat. The victims of the Seventh Syndicate human trafficking were in there, and it was Olesk's job to move them to the airfield. "We're on," she told Arash. If Olesk was listening, it wouldn't set off any alarms for him. But Arash received her meaning and set his jaw.

She was about to text Vincent the address and information on the location when a message came in from Olesk. "Keep moving. We're to go four blocks north and circle in a holding pattern."

As Arash took them past the movie theater, she caught a glimpse of Olesk's car in an alley a block away. Olesk sat, expressionless behind the wheel, with Ellie next to him in the passenger seat. Once Stephanie and Arash were clear from view, she messaged Vincent the address. He replied quickly: I'll be there. 20 min? On official business with local officers. They've been informed that I have people on the inside.

The two cargo vans driven by Thom and Hector passed Arash and Stephanie, heading toward the movie theater. Her gut clenched thinking about those terrified people who would soon be shackled to those seats. Arash shifted, rolling his shoulders and showing his frustration. He fumed for revenge, and she wondered if he'd be able to control that desire until the right moment.

As soon as Arash pulled up to a curb and idled she showed him the message from Vincent. Arash checked his watch. She knew that twenty minutes would be too long. Arash asked, "You have eyes on David?"

"Haven't seen him, probably orbiting closer."

A new message arrived from Olesk. She read it aloud. "Loaded. Head north. Maintain your perimeter. Eyes open. You're the first line of defense."

"No address." Arash pulled onto the street and aimed them north.

"Not until the last minute." By then it would be too late to inform Vincent and the FBI. She turned in her seat to look behind and spotted the two vans moving slowly along a street. "They're rolling." Olesk darted past the vans and disappeared. David's Chevy lurked farther in the distance.

Arash watched the rearview mirror more than the road ahead. "We can't let them scatter." He pulled hard on the wheel and into a tight U-turn. The engine revved and she saw the energy growing in him, too. But could just the two of them end this?

Another sedan moved on pace with the white vans. It was Grant Hemmings's car. "The Seventh is here." Her pulse raced knowing that the time had to be now. "Go," she urged Arash with a whisper.

He didn't need much encouragement to rocket the mini-van forward. Up ahead, the two cargo vans separated, one of them turning up a side street. It wouldn't be long before they were all too strung out along the roads to contain.

Arash aimed at the remaining van. David lurked two blocks behind it. Stephanie messaged Vincent. Now. He replied: Inbound. It looked like Arash was going to take them right into the nose of the van. At the last second, he skidded to the side. Their modifications to the suspension handled it perfectly, but her heart still thundered.

The van screeched to a stop, blocked by Arash and Stephanie. She saw Thom behind the windshield, hands raised and eyes wide asking what the hell was going on. Arash turned to her. "Take the wheel." He leaped out of the minivan and hurried toward Thom. She slid into the driver's seat and strapped in. The fuse was lit. All the secrets were about to explode.

ARASH RAN TOWARD the driver's side of the white cargo van, pointing vaguely up the street. "They're coming," he called to Thom.

Thom rolled the window down. "Who?"

"You didn't see them?" Arash's muscles blazed, ready. "Let me drive."

"Hell, no. That's not part of the plan." Thom waved at Stephanie to get out of the way.

"The plan was screwed the second you killed Marcos." Arash put his hands on the edge of the open driver's-side window.

Thom shuddered, confused. "Wait. What?" His eyes went wide when Arash reached into the van, grabbed him by his heavy flannel shirt and dragged him out of the window. Arash threw him down to the street. Thom rolled and came up with a knife in his hand. He charged Arash. "I always knew you were a son of a—"

Arash's knife was already out. He had to move without thinking to survive. He swiped his forearm across Thom's wrist, redirecting his attack, and buried his own blade in Thom's ribs. For a moment he held Thom standing, then let him fall to the ground. Sirens pierced the cold air. Thom writhed and Arash leaned over him. "If you live, you'll rot in jail."

A motor growled from a block away. David's Chevy

approached. Arash threw the door open on the van and got behind the wheel. Stephanie sped away in the minivan and he peeled off behind her. Small voices wept behind him. His heart froze when he glanced back through the barricade he'd installed and saw the terrified faces of sixteen young boys and girls of different ethnicities who ranged in age from what looked like ten years old up into the teens. "You're safe now," he promised with a choked voice. "You're safe." But no one was yet.

David rumbled closer in the Chevy. Stephanie tuned hard and away from Arash. As she curled around to cut off David, Arash saw her pointing in the direction of the coming sirens. Her friends were almost there. Before David could catch up to Arash, Stephanie swept past his front bumper, causing him to slam on his brakes. She nimbly doubled back and came at David again. The muscle car churned hard and powered away before she T-boned him.

A block over to the right, Arash spotted three black SUVs with light bars flashing at the tops of their windshields. He angled toward them and honked repeatedly when he was just a few yards away. The SUVs came to a stop in a tactical formation and the doors opened. Arash stepped from the van with his hands raised calling out, "Bolt cutters. There are kids back here."

One man in an FBI windbreaker stepped forward, lowering his pistol. He was dark complected and spoke with clear authority. "Stand down. He's with me." The man waved the others forward. "And get those bolt cutters." Once the man was close to Arash, he spoke in low tones. "I'm Vincent. Friend of Stephanie's."

The other FBI agents threw open the van doors and were confronted by the scared faces of sixteen young boys and girls. Ellie's voice came over the comm in the van. "What the hell is going on?"

Arash burned to move. "Stephanie's still out there."

Vincent held up his keys. "Take mine."

Arash glanced at the cumbersome tank of an SUV. He knew the mods of the cargo van outpaced it. "This'll do better. Get me back on the road."

Vincent joined a female agent carrying a pair of bolt cutters and the two of them rushed to the van. Arash jumped into the driver's seat as the shackles were being cut from the rings welded to the seats. With a gentle voice Vincent guided the boys and girls out. "This way. You're safe now with the authorities and I will make sure that nothing happens to you."

Hector's voice crackled on the comm. "I have no idea. Thom, check in." All of the kids were out of the van and Arash stepped on the gas with the side door gaping open. Hector continued. "Thom. Thom?"

Arash picked up the comm and impersonated Thom's voice as best he could. "What's your twenty?"

Hector answered, "About ten blocks up from pickup, on the side street parallel to the main drag."

Standing on the accelerator, Arash ate up the streets. Up and to the right, he saw Stephanie take the minivan in a tight circle while avoiding a charge from David. The car Stephanie had identified as part of the Seventh Syndicate edged on the perimeter, as if uncertain how to get involved.

Arash gritted his teeth and aimed for the rear fender of the Syndicate sedan. It was too late by the time the driver saw him coming. A direct impact had the potential to disable the van, so Arash yanked the wheel to the side and skidded the side of the van into the rear of the sedan. Glass and plastic shattered and rained into the open van. Arash jarred hard in his seat and gripped the steering wheel with all his strength to stay in place. The driver of the sedan wasn't as strong and struck his head into the side window.

The van was still operational and rolled forward. The side of the sedan was crushed around its rear wheel and could only limp for a foot before halting. As he sped away, Arash caught a glimpse of Stephanie in the minivan speeding toward the sedan. He knew how good a driver she was, but he still tightened with concern seeing her in the middle of the grinding danger. Whatever he was about to do next, he had to do it fast and get to her side.

"Status." Ellie came over the comm. "Status!"

Hector was the first to respond. "Proceeding on plan. No sign of Thom... There he is." Arash was a half block away from Hector. He got up alongside and saw Hector still holding the comm mic. "What the hell—" Hector's voice over the speaker was cut off when Arash pulled in front of him and slammed on the brakes.

Hector tried to reverse, but Arash was faster and swung his van around to pin his vehicle next to a telephone pole. Hector slammed out of the driver's side, flexing his thick arms. "What are you doing?"

"Same thing I did to Thom." Arash swung a fist at Hector, but the other man dodged to the side. Hector bull-rushed Arash and crashed into his body, knocking the wind out of him. The two men stumbled into the middle of the street. Arash gathered his breath and separated himself enough to drive a knee into Hector's ribs. He followed it with a punch to the jaw that sent Hector backward. Arash closed the distance and drove a fist into Hector's gut.

Hector curled his hands into Arash's coat and wheezed, "You're a damn rat."

"No." Arash took hold of Hector's jacket and yanked him close. "I'm a friend of Marcos."

"Marcos?" Hector's eyes went wide as the information struck him. He tried to twist from Arash's grip, but Arash held strong and swung Hector into the street just as David was charging up toward them. Tires screamed and the impact took Hector to the asphalt. David swung wide away from the accident and sped up a separate street.

Arash ran to Hector's van and climbed behind the wheel. Another sixteen kids. More terrified eyes and barely suppressed sobs. Arash scraped the side of this van against the other as he took it onto the street. "You'll be okay," he tried to reassure the kids. To the right, near a long line of warehouses, Stephanie parked next to the Seventh Syndicate man's broken car. A couple blocks beyond her was one of the FBI SUVs.

And ahead of Arash was Olesk's car. All hell had broken loose and Arash could finally make him burn.

Chapter Twenty-One

Stephanie hauled a dazed Grant Hemmings out of his car and helped him stand. "I've got you." She really wanted to put her fist in his throat and hand him over to Vincent and the FBI, but the situation was still completely unstable. Sirens blared a couple blocks away, too far for her to drag Grant.

One block to her left, Arash pulled away in the second cargo van. She'd watched him fight with Hector and nearly get run down by David in the process. She also saw what his target was now. Olesk. But Arash had a van full of victims. How far would his need for revenge take him?

"Oh, thank God," Grant slurred. "Get us out of here." She threw open the side door of the minivan and let him tumble onto the third-row seat. He was swiveling to look out all the windows while mumbling, "The FBI? We paid our guy. Who could've called this in?"

She looked to where Arash was as she got into the driver's seat, but he was already gone. Every screeching tire made her heart leap into her throat. Every second was life or death for her and Arash.

Stephanie shot the minivan forward and sped toward the last place she'd seen the FBI cars, but a dark presence cut her off. David veered just in front of the minivan and she swerved just in time to not get taken out. The Chevy swung around, piling black smoke behind it, then sped at her. She raced away and searched for any advantage against the more powerful car.

"Isn't he with us?" Grant stared out the back window. "I've met him. What the hell is going on?"

Stephanie answered by veering hard to one side of the street. Grant slid across the bench seat and slammed into the sidewall. His eyes spun and he scrambled to grasp the nearest seat belt. Her move had thrown David for a second. He corrected and sped closer again. She took the minivan into a quick left turn that brought Grant hard into the opposite side of the minivan.

David pursued, face furious in the rearview mirror. He was angling her farther away from where she'd last seen Vincent and the FBI. With the Seventh Syndicate man as her cargo, her mission was so close to being complete. But the kids were still out there with Arash, his fate completely unknown.

The minivan rocked hard and the steering wheel was jarred from her grip. David had rammed them and was recoiling to do it again. She got the wheel back in her sore hands and righted the minivan before it fishtailed too hard. Her muscles burned as she regained control while plotting her next move. Instead of gaining speed, she slowed as if the minivan was still lost in a skid. She pulled it into a sideways drift and fought the forces trying to yank her out of her seat.

The side of the minivan would be the perfect prey for David. He bit at the bait she presented and his engine screamed. He sped closer with all the muscle under his hood. She pulled out of the drift and straightened out. He shot past the minivan, hopped a curb, lost contact with the ground and smashed down into the side of a loading dock. The car crumpled, nearly folding in half, spraying fluids and hissing smoke.

"Hey!" Grant shouted from the back seat. "Stop the car and tell me exactly what is going on." He pointed a pistol at her.

OLESK. FINALLY. ARASH could end it. The van had the power to catch him while he was this close.

But the victims weren't safe. Their terror clouded the air and Arash couldn't breathe. Taking out Thom and Hector hadn't brought Marcos back. There'd been no voice from the cloudless sky thanking Arash for his revenge, or forgiving him for not being able to save Marcos. His friend's hopes and dreams had ended and nothing he did now could change that.

But there were sixteen humans in the van who still had a chance.

Arash steered away from Olesk and toward the FBI. Stephanie in the minivan blurred between warehouses a couple blocks away, pursued by David. Arash pushed the van as fast as it could go, his blood burning white-hot.

"Status." Ellie's worried voice came over the comm. "Status!"

Arash pulled to a stop among two of the FBI SUVs. He didn't bother getting out of the van this time. Vincent knew the drill and got his Feds to quickly free the kids in the cargo area. "That's it," Vincent said, relieved. "They're safe."

"Stephanie," Arash gritted. "Stephanie." He peeled away to find her.

Ellie kept trying through the comm, sounding more desperate. "Somebody come back with your status."

Arash picked up the mic. "Thom and Hector are gone." He saw the minivan in the distance. Stephanie pulled a perfect drift, then snapped straight as David swept past her. The Chevy disappeared next to a warehouse, but from the sound of screaming metal, Arash knew the outcome. "David's gone."

Olesk's voice came over the speaker with a warning. "Arash…"

"You're next, Olesk." Arash wished he was squeezing

Olesk's throat instead of the mic. "You're next because you took money to drive these kids to hell. You're next because you killed Marcos." He threw the mic down and drove to where he'd last seen Stephanie.

There she was, intact and still driving. But any relief that started to wash over him chilled when he saw the Seventh Syndicate man in the back of the minivan, pistol outstretched toward Stephanie.

No. Arash should be in that car with her. No.

She slammed on the brakes and ducked. The man's chest crushed into the back of the seat in front of him. The gun went off and pain flashed through Arash as if he'd been hit. But the bullet flew through the cabin and punched a hole in the front windshield.

Stephanie quickly lunged from the driver's seat to the rear of the minivan. Arash brought his van alongside and jumped out before it stopped rolling. The man tried to raise the pistol again, but Stephanie twisted it from his grip and it spun to the floor toward the front of the car.

Arash threw the side door of the minivan open and planted his fist in the face of the man. The man sprawled backward, then collapsed forward. When he rose up again, he had a smaller revolver in his hand. It swung toward Stephanie and Arash wrapped both hands around it, trapping the hammer.

Stephanie moved in a blur, snapping a knife out and driving the blade into the man's thigh, just above the knee. The man screamed, hands going limp to release the gun into Arash's grip. The deepest betrayal carved into the man's eyes as he stared at Stephanie. She faced him, unmoved. "You're finished."

A siren blasted behind them. Arash grabbed the man's lapels and yanked him out of the minivan. Vincent pulled up in his SUV just as Arash was dropping the Seventh Syndicate man to the concrete.

"Olesk." Stephanie pointed up between the rows of industrial buildings. The Subaru sped over the streets. If it hit the highways, it could be gone in a flash. Arash charged through the side door of the minivan and into the driver's seat. Stephanie leaped into the passenger seat, determined. "End this."

The wind howled through the open side door as Arash bolted them toward Olesk. Arash reached out and Stephanie took hold of his hand. Fear and fury had numbed him until this touch. New life arced through him. "You alright?" he asked.

"Yeah." She nodded. "You?"

"Still driving." He saw her attention was on the sideview mirror and he checked behind them. Vincent stood over the Seventh Syndicate man. Arash said, "You got him."

"We did." She focused forward. "We're not done." Olesk was still a couple of blocks ahead of them and approaching a freeway on-ramp. Wringing all the speed he could from the minivan, Arash blasted across the asphalt toward Olesk. Stephanie braced herself on the door handle and scanned the area around them. "Olesk drives like a machine. Throw something completely unexpected at him. He won't be able to process it."

The Subaru curved up the on-ramp. Arash blew through a red light and wove between two crossing cars. Their surprised horns faded quickly in the distance as he charged onto the freeway. Arash pulled close enough to see Ellie in the passenger seat, preparing Olesk's pistol. Instead of dropping back, Arash built more speed and passed Olesk while he was jammed in a small knot of traffic.

As soon as Olesk cleared the other cars, he gained quickly on Arash and Stephanie. Arash raced him into an interchange in the freeway with multiple curving ramps at different levels. "Hold on," Arash warned. Stephanie braced herself and Arash slammed on the brakes in the middle of a curving ramp. The minivan slowed hard on the custom brakes and slid a little sideways.

Olesk wove with indecision, braking at first, then chirping his tires for more speed. Arash stepped on the gas again as soon as Olesk was beside them and jammed the minivan toward the Subaru. Olesk yanked his car away, head turning wildly as he tried to adjust to the changing landscape of the freeway around them. He didn't have a chance. His car slammed into a guardrail, scattering chips of concrete. The churning tires caught and rocketed the car farther forward, up over the rail and down the twenty-foot drop from the interchange ramp.

Arash drove on. Below him and Stephanie, Olesk's car lay on its crushed roof among overgrown weeds.

It was over.

Marcos wasn't alive again. But thirty-two people were free from harm. The Seventh Syndicate was hurt. And Stephanie was safe next to Arash.

While they were still moving, she got out of her seat and closed the side door. He throttled back into the flow of traffic. The minivan dissolved from suspicion. After a mile, he realized he didn't know where he was going. "Navigate?"

Stephanie pulled out her phone. "Message from Vincent. He says they have it contained and the victims are safe." She sighed long. "I'm telling him that we're gone." After typing she put the phone in the center console. "Take us back to Vegas. I need a room." She reached out and ran her fingers over the back of his neck. He was still alive. "With you. I need to breathe again."

He vowed, "I will take you anywhere you want to go."

She turned to him, dark eyes shining. "I want to go anywhere with you."

Epilogue

Air tools ratcheted in quick percussion, metal clanged against metal and voices rose above the din. It was music. The smells of motor oil and tire rubber added to Stephanie's feast. She leaned against a desk on one side of Arash's new garage and watched as he instructed a young black woman on the parts under Mariana Balducci's hoisted pickup truck.

All three of the bays in the garage were full and two more cars were parked on the driveway on the other side of the open doors. Everything from oil changes to new water pumps. And if anyone from the Oakland neighborhood wandered in, they were sure to get a lesson on whatever was being done. The garage hadn't turned a financial profit, but the benefit to Stephanie and Arash, to the neighborhood and the city, went way beyond the financial. People were able to stay on the road and make a living. And the next generation of mechanics were having their curiosity fed.

Ty Morrison stood at the desk next to Stephanie. Instead of the usual suit he wore as the police chief of his town, he was in casual flannel and jeans. Stephanie could see the resemblance between Ty and his stern ancestor in the old Frontier Justice photographs from the nineteenth century. Two black men with unmovable resolve. But Ty was actually smiling. "Hemmings's trial is starting soon. Looks like he'll go away for a long time. And the info you tracked down during the operation has the Seventh scrambling.

Their human trafficking is over and they're scared." It had been two months since San Pedro. "Vincent said the FBI has cleaned some house and is really going after them now."

Ty really lit up when Mariana came into the garage. He stepped to meet her and gave her a kiss that lasted just a little longer than proper. But Stephanie wasn't going to shut them down. She and Arash had been caught during several lingering kisses on the porch of Mariana's farmhouse, which also served as the Frontier Justice home base. Usually it was Vincent who cleared his throat with some embarrassment. If Javier was around, he'd just grumble and stalk off to the orchard.

Mariana had a tray of four cups of coffee and handed two to Stephanie and Ty. She motioned to Arash with the other and showed him where she put it on the desk. He gave her a wave, then caught Stephanie's eye. She warmed, even though spring hadn't made it to the Bay Area. Arash finished up with the girl he was teaching and came over to Stephanie and the others. Stephanie's blush grew higher when he leaned down and kissed her on the cheek. Even the smallest touch was electric. Something she'd discovered when Arash had brushed his fingers against hers under the table during a generally comfortable dinner with her father and mother.

After taking a drink, Mariana wound an arm around Ty's waist and stood close. "How does the truck look?"

"Nothing major." Stephanie had looked it over initially with Arash.

"Maybe new brakes." Arash nodded. "But Stephanie secured us a deal with a manufacturer to subsidize parts."

Ty grew serious. "You're doing good for the people out here."

"There's always something to fix." Arash looked out over the garage, but she knew he was talking about more than just the cars. Between the intel gathered by Frontier Justice, her network, and the information that slipped through the neighborhood into the garage, they were all aware that the Seventh Syndicate and other forces that preyed on disadvantaged people might be quiet, but they weren't dead.

Arash wasn't daunted. After seeing the lives he'd saved in the vans, and learning that mourning Marcos was about more than revenge, he'd joined Frontier Justice and made the organization that much more formidable. She understood his strength, and felt it in the light of day and the darkest times at night. She'd seen the same determination in his parents the moment she'd met them. That dedication ran through Ty, Mariana and the others. Stephanie knew that none of them would quit. Even against what looked like impossible odds. They'd survived, and would again. It was a fight they could win because they all stood together.

* * * * *

COMING SOON!

We really hope you enjoyed reading this book. If you're looking for more romance, be sure to head to the shops when new books are available on

Thursday 4th April

To see which titles are coming soon, please visit

millsandboon.co.uk/nextmonth